DEADLY DOLL

Tinker stepped out onto the shimmering energy bridge. He looked down at the canyon floor, and his stomach knotted.

From the opposite side the evil Dedstorm advanced. "It's a long way to fall, isn't it? I do hope you won't slip," the villain sneered.

With a flash, a ball of light appeared between Dedstorm's palms, and an energy bolt shot out. With lightning speed, Tinker raised his hands palms outward and dispersed the energy.

"You'll pay for that!" Dedstorm vowed. He shrank the bridge, narrowing it into nothing.

"Dedstorm!" Tinker called out. "If I fall, we both fall!" He shot a stream of pure energy at the machine projecting the bridge.

"No, you fool!" Dedstorm cried. "You'll overload it!"

With that, the energy bridge winked out. For half a heartbeat, Tinker and Dedstorm seemed to be hanging in midair. Then they were both hurtling downward to be smashed on the jagged rocks below.

Books in the Tom Swift® Series

#1 THE BLACK DRAGON
#2 THE NEGATIVE ZONE
#3 CYBORG KICKBOXER
#4 THE DNA DISASTER
#5 MONSTER MACHINE
#6 AQUATECH WARRIORS
#7 MOONSTALKER
#8 THE MICROBOTS
#9 FIRE BIKER
#10 MIND GAMES

A Hardy Boys & Tom Swift Ultra Thriller

TIME BOMB

Available from ARCHWAY Paperbacks

TOM SWIFT 10

MIND GAMES

VICTOR APPLETON

AN ARCHWAY PAPERBACK
Published by POCKET BOOKS
New York   London   Toronto   Sydney   Tokyo   Singapore

AN ARCHWAY PAPERBACK *Original*

An Archway Paperback published by
POCKET BOOKS, a division of Simon & Schuster Inc.
1230 Avenue of the Americas, New York, NY 10020

Copyright © 1992 by Simon & Schuster Inc.

Produced by Byron Preiss Visual Publications, Inc.

ISBN: 0-671-75654-0

First Archway Paperback printing October 1992

10 9 8 7 6 5 4 3 2 1

TOM SWIFT, AN ARCHWAY PAPERBACK and colophon
are registered trademarks of Simon & Schuster Inc.

Cover art by Romas Kukalis

Printed in the U.S.A.

IL 6+

MIND GAMES

THIS IS FANTASTIC!" TOM SWIFT EXCLAIMED. "I'M IN an alien world, and I'm the first to experience it."

Peering through a thick glass portal, Tom took in the strangely beautiful view of the mid-Atlantic rift. Five miles below the surface of the ocean was truly a place no one had gone before. Tom watched in fascination as thick streams of steam bubbles rose from sea floor vents and flowed along the walls of the undersea canyon he was exploring. Hundreds of huge feather worms that were anchored to the ocean bottom waved in the hot currents created by the escaping gases.

Tom was testing one of his newest inventions, the supersubmersible officially known as a Drilling, Depth-Intensive Vent Explorer—or DIVE for short. He had designed the DIVE to drill into the

1

sea floor at places where new mantle emerged from beneath the floor to renew the surface of the earth in a never-ending process. Beyond the reach of the DIVE's banks of halogen lights, the rest of the unexplored world remained hidden from view.

"What an incredible sight," Tom said. "It's like watching the birth of the planet. Are you getting all of this, Alan?"

"Yes, Tom. I see it on my monitor." A faraway voice came through the DIVE's internal speakers. It belonged to Tom's friend Alan Lee. In this experiment, Alan was acting as remote supervisor, watching the exploratory drilling operation from a distant control center.

"You'd better keep your mind on business, Tom," Alan warned. "This is where the drilling gets really dangerous. Remember, the object of this experiment is to drill deep enough to tap the earth's internal heat without opening a hole that will spew lava. You're trying to create the world's first controlled deep-sea thermal generator—not the world's first man-made volcano."

Tom smiled. "Right, Alan," he said, keeping his gaze on the fantastic world outside the DIVE. The thick glass of the portal reflected Tom's image back at him. In the dim blue light of the on-board computer screens, Tom's blond hair looked ghostly white.

"Wow. Now, that's a great detail," he muttered.

"What did you say, Tom?"

Tom shook his head, looking into the console

minicam so that Alan could see his grin. "Sorry, Alan. I was talking to myself."

Then Tom grew serious and returned his attention to the controls of the DIVE's drill. One of the monitor screens showed him the drill's progress as it plunged through the hard basalt of the ocean floor. The earth's crust along the mid-Atlantic trench was thin but incredibly hard. Tom did not need to be reminded that drilling into it, inching closer to the molten rock below, was dangerous work. He was also aware of the staggering pressure surrounding him and the experimental sub. Six tons of pressure per square inch threatened to crush the DIVE and Tom into a thin, gooey film of metal and flesh.

Tom saw from his instrument panel that the drill bit was close to optimum depth. The air inside the small submersible was humid, and Tom felt droplets of moisture beading on his face and forearms. He wasn't sure if this was condensation from the air or nervous perspiration from the knowledge that he was drilling so close to molten rock.

Checking the drill's depth monitor, Tom said, "I'm just three degrees Celsius from reaching the target temperature." One of the exterior TV monitors showed Tom the drill shaft as it disappeared into the hole it had dug. Streams of tiny bubbles flew from the hole. "I'm getting some steam bubbles now. Check out monitor three."

"Got it," Alan said. "Looks like the fizz from a bottle of warm soda."

"Well, it's not anything you'd want to drink." Tom said. "Do you have any idea how hot that water must be?"

"For water to boil at this depth, with a pressure of six tons per square inch, the temperature has to be . . ." Alan paused to do some quick calculations, then said, "Real hot, Tom. Really, really hot."

"Thank you for your scientific exactness." Tom laughed.

At that moment a low hum sounded through the length of the DIVE. Tom felt the floor shake beneath his feet. The threatening vibration continued to grow, and Tom quickly cut the drill's speed, bringing it to a complete stop. Despite himself, his voice was a bit shaky as he asked, "What was that?"

"Hang on," Alan said, trying to keep his own voice calm. "I'm getting the remote analysis from Megatron right now."

Megatron was the supercomputer at the heart of Swift Enterprises. It controlled many of the daily automatic operations, ran the fusion reactor, distributed power throughout the complex, and analyzed data from the numerous experiments that were conducted each day.

"Uh, Tom, maybe we should cut the experiment short. We have a lot of data now. I think we should analyze it and then make a second trip down with the DIVE. The drill hole won't go anywhere."

"Why, Alan? What is Megatron reporting?"

"Well, Tom, those deep vibrations you just felt

were identical to those generated just before an earthquake."

Tom wiped the sweat from his upper lip and checked the temperature readouts again. "We're only one degree away from our target. It seems a shame to pull out now. Just a little more drilling, and we'll have a new source of limitless energy—superheated steam from the heart of the earth."

"Maybe so, but I don't like what I'm seeing, Tom," Alan replied. On his remote monitor, he watched as the stream of superheated gas bubbles flooded out of the drill hole with increasing volume.

Checking his on-board monitor, Tom saw it, too. But he shook his head, saying, "We're too close. This is no time to stop. Besides, what have we got to lose?"

"Aside from your life and a five-million-dollar experimental vehicle, why, nothing at all," Alan said with a sigh. He knew that tone in Tom's voice meant that the young inventor would not cut and run.

As he started up the drill again Tom said, "I really don't think we'll lose the DIVE, Alan. Besides, I can always detach the sub from the drill and make for safer waters. Everything is under control. Really."

"Famous last words," Alan shot back. "Don't forget that the canyon you're in doesn't give the sub much room to maneuver."

Tom didn't respond. Instead he gave his full attention to the drill controls. Slowly the drill bit dug into deeper and hotter layers of bedrock. For the next few minutes there were no quakes or vibrations. Tom kept drilling at a steady speed until a green light flashed on his control panel.

"All right, Tom! You did it!" Alan's voice gushed over the sub's speakers. "The experiment's a success! It's over. You can come on home now."

"Only one part of the experiment is over," Tom said softly. "Now for phase two. In order to test the DIVE completely, I need to see how well it functions in an emergency—how easily the drill can be detached and how maneuverable the DIVE is without it."

Tom moved a lever that increased the speed of the drill. It was now spinning faster than design tolerances specified. Red warning lights began to flash all over the small submersible. A buzzer sounded, and an electronic voice warned: "Drill motor overload. Reduce speed. Reduce speed!"

"Tom, what are you doing?" Alan asked, panic creeping into his voice.

"I'm trying to max out the DIVE, that's what!"

"Tom, your judgment must be affected by the depth and the pressure. This is not safe. Detach the drill now, and begin your ascent immediately!"

"Too bad Rick Cantwell isn't here," Tom said calmly. "He's always lived by one motto: Test to destruction."

"Tom! A warning from Megatron—your drilling is setting up harmonic vibrations in the rock walls around you, as well as in the crust. Stress fractures have appeared. You're moments away from caving in the canyon walls—if the sea floor doesn't turn into a live volcano first!"

Now Tom could feel the building vibrations. Suddenly the floor of the DIVE began to tilt downward. Then Tom felt and heard what sounded like an explosion on the outer hull of the small sub.

"Tom! The canyon walls are giving way. Get out of there!"

A few boulders bounced off the DIVE's hull. The sound inside was deafening. Tom quickly pushed a whole bank of levers. "All right, Alan. I've detached the drill. I'm coming up!"

"Give it all the power you've got left, Tom," Alan said tightly. "Oh, no! Look at the drill hole!" Alan's voice transmission was now half drowned out by static.

As he struggled with the controls of the DIVE to get it to rise, Tom angled a camera down to see what Alan was talking about. Pushing out of the drill hole and melting the steel-alloy shaft of the abandoned drill was a thick black mass accompanied by huge clouds of steam bubbles. As Tom watched, he saw the blackness crack open, revealing an intense white-orange glow inside.

"Tom! It's—"

"Lava. Yes, I know, Alan. Uh, the external stresses seem to have caught up to the DIVE. I'm at full power, but I'm not getting any lift." Tom spoke quietly, determined not to panic as he gave his full attention to the emergency control panel. The craft started to rise just as more boulders came crashing down on top of it. The DIVE stopped rising and began to fall again.

Tom's vision was suddenly blurred by a spray of scalding hot water—a leak had sprung in the roof of the sub. He ignored it, gunning all power to the DIVE's emergency jet system. Still the sub continued to sink. With a horrible scraping sound, it settled into the searing lava bed below. Through the floor, Tom felt the heat of the molten rock. Above him, water shot through another fracture in the sub's hull. Then his control panel went dark, and the lights failed. The sizzling lava was destroying the sub's batteries.

Tom could feel that the hot water pouring in was already up to his knees. He pushed buttons and levers, hoping to get some response from the dying craft. Nothing happened. He smashed his fist down on the control panel in sheer frustration. "Looks like I have my choice of death. I can fry like a clam, get boiled like a lobster, or drown."

The small sub's support beams groaned and twisted. Tom heard a metallic warping noise. In the dark, to no one in particular, he said, "Oh, yeah. I forgot about the possibility of being crushed to death."

Then, with an earsplitting roar, the entire ceiling of the minisub collapsed.

BLACKNESS. SILENCE. TOM FELT FROZEN IN A MO-
ment outside of time. Then, like the rush of a distant waterfall, came the static of white noise. The
blackness surrounding Tom turned grainy, then
brightened into the snow of a dead TV channel.
The white noise grew louder, and Tom's skin tin-
gled. His scalp itched.

In the snowy space before him, green letters materialized: Simulation Over.

Through the static, Tom heard Alan's voice.
"Tom, are you okay?"

I'm *not* dead, Tom thought. His heart was
pounding. He tried to move and felt the weight of
an enormous helmet on his head. Raising a shaking hand to his face, he touched the black visor
that covered his eyes.

"Tom!" Alan cried more urgently.

Even though he couldn't see anything but the Simulation Over message, Tom could feel a switch on his armrest. He flipped it, and the snow, white noise, and tingling stopped. The huge helmet rose straight up, and Tom blinked in the glare of fluorescent lights.

On the other side of a glass wall, Alan Lee was on the edge of his seat. A dozen TV monitors flickered around him, but his eyes were on Tom. Tom looked at the chrome and black leather chair he was sitting in. He had known he wasn't really five miles beneath the ocean's surface. He hadn't even left his laboratory at Swift Enterprises. But the entire simulation, including death, had been very convincing. Tom's body was still reacting with symptoms of shock.

"I'm okay," Tom assured his friend, getting out of the ergonomic chair. But as he tried to stand, his knees buckled.

Alan was out of the control room and at his side in an instant. "Should I alert the medical team?"

Tom shook his head. "Dying just takes some getting used to, Alan." He managed a shaky grin. "Now, what do you think of my new invention, the Total Reality Generator?"

Alan looked at the helmet and chair. "It's the most incredible simulator I've ever seen," he said. "But is it safe? I mean, look at the condition you're in."

"As long as you don't die in simulation, you

come out feeling terrific," Tom assured him. "Want to try it?"

Alan gave the machine a doubtful look. "First I want to know how this thing works."

Well, Tom thought, that was Alan for you. Both he and Rick Cantwell were interested in Tom's inventions, but Alan had a more technical mind. Rick's questions often started and ended with, "How fast can it go before it breaks?"

"Let me give you a demonstration," Tom said, leaning shakily against the back of the chair. "Have a seat."

"I don't know about this, Tom."

Tom patted the oversize black helmet. "I just told you, it's harmless as long as you don't die in simulation."

Alan sat gingerly. After making a few adjustments so that the chair supported his friend evenly, Tom lowered the black helmet over Alan's head. The opaque visor covered Alan's eyes.

Tom toggled an armrest switch.

"Hey!" Alan said. "That itches!"

"You'll feel that when the sensors contact your scalp. It'll go away in a minute." Tom hurried behind the glass wall and sat at the TRG's controls.

"Megatron," he said, bringing the computer's voice-activated system on-line.

"Ready," said the computer.

"Rerun the previous simulation," Tom commanded, "from where the drill is three degrees below target temperature."

"Understood," the computer said. "Beginning simulation from that point . . . now."

The TV monitors sprang to life. One monitor showed the drill shaft disappearing into the sea floor. Another showed the view outside the DIVE's starboard portal. On a third monitor Tom could see Alan standing at the DIVE's controls.

Alan blinked and touched the controls uncertainly. "Tom?" he said. "Can you hear me?"

"Loud and clear," Tom said, smiling. He knew Alan would be a little disoriented. It was one thing to see a TRG simulation from the control room, but now the simulation was inside Alan's head. "What do you think?"

"It's weird. One minute I was sitting in that chair, and then suddenly I'm here." On the screen, Alan jumped up and down, making the metal floor ring beneath his feet.

"Your real body, here in the lab, looks perfectly still," Tom said. "Actually, your muscles are moving—infinitesimally. The TRG helmet stimulates the brain directly and screens out most of the nerve impulses that would make you really move. Now I want you to notice something. Look at the portal and tell me what you see."

"Pretty much what I expect," Alan said. "I've got a view of the steam vent. There are bubbles coming out. And on the rocks along the sides are those worm things."

"Feather worms. Keep looking. What else do you notice?"

The image of Alan frowned. Then he raised his eyebrows. "Oh, I see my reflection." He laughed. "I'm wearing a jumpsuit with a Swift Enterprises logo."

"I didn't program the reflection in. Megatron figured it out, understanding that the glass, under the programmed lighting conditions, would reflect. That's why it's so easy to program the TRG. I can tell Megatron part of what the simulation is supposed to do, and the fuzzy logic circuits figure out the rest."

"Wow, you've got fuzzy logic built into Megatron?"

Tom grinned, knowing that, as a computer programming whiz, Alan would appreciate the cutting edge in computer technology. "As you know," Tom continued, "fuzzy logic circuits allow a computer to think not just in the realm of ones and zeroes, but in the fuzzy region between those absolutes. Fuzzy logic gives Megatron the power to imitate human creativity.

"I haven't shown you the best feature of all," Tom added. "Run the drill for a while without talking to me, and I'll show you what I mean."

Tom turned off his microphone, then toggled a switch that was labeled Speed of Simulation.

On the screen, Alan moved at high speed, as though he were in a fast-motion movie. Tom watched for a while, then toggled the switch again. Alan slowed down to normal speed, and Tom turned the microphone on again.

"I'm back, Alan," he said. "How long do you think it's been since I last spoke to you?"

"About ten minutes," Alan answered. "Listen, I'm two degrees from the drill's target temperature, but I'm starting to get vibrations." On the screen, the DIVE shook.

Tom looked at his watch. "Alan, I last spoke to you sixty seconds ago."

"Tom, what should I do about these vibrations?"

"Forget 'em for a minute. Aren't you impressed with the high-speed simulation feature? What seemed like ten minutes to you was only a tenth of that in real time. That's the other big advantage of the TRG. It may be more expensive to build than any other simulator, but it can teach people much faster. A student pilot can experience an hour of flight time in six minutes."

"Great," Alan said dismissively. "Now tell me if I ought to keep drilling. A rock just tumbled down the canyon wall. Things are getting hairy down here!" On the screen, Alan's face was grim.

"Alan, it's only a simulation."

"Yeah, yeah. But do I keep drilling or not?"

On the monitor, Tom could see the intensity in Alan's eyes. Alan looked obsessed, totally absorbed by the simulation. "I'm bringing you up," Tom said.

"No!" Alan protested, but the helmet was already rising from his head. In the chair, he turned and looked at Tom. "How could you do that? I was just getting into it!"

Tom came out of the control room. "I just want to make a quick adjustment so that I can show you another feature." He opened a panel in the helmet's side and started to work, adding casually, "How do you feel?"

"Like I want to get back to the simulation," Alan said. "Another couple of minutes and I'll hit the target temperature. I just hope I can get out of there when I do. This beats your average video game, that's for sure!"

Video games, Tom thought, somewhat reassured. Of course Alan would look obsessed in the midst of such a convincing and dramatic simulation. It was like the ultimate video game. Still, Alan's intensity had been a little disturbing, as though he'd been losing touch with reality.

"Speaking of games," Alan continued, "have you considered programming the TRG for Galaxy Masters?"

Tom smiled. Galaxy Masters was the fantasy role-playing game invented by Jefferson High School student Les Hempel and his father. Tom and his friends, along with half of Jefferson High, had been test-playing the game. In fact, the game was so much fun that a double-elimination tournament had been organized, even though Galaxy Masters was still only in the testing stage. The tournament had been going on for two weeks and was now down to two teams. Tom and Alan's team was one of them.

"No," Tom said, still working on the helmet.

"Why not?" Alan asked. "Can't the TRG simulate something as complex as Galaxy Masters?"

Tom didn't like the idea of using the TRG to simulate a game, but Alan's question propelled him into a quick mental review of the game's parameters. There were two parts to each team—four heroes and a villain—just as a football team had both offensive and defensive players. The heroes were challenged to defeat the villain of an opposing team. The team member who played the villain challenged the four heroes of the other team.

The goal of the villainous character, Dedstorm, was to activate an ancient army of drone weapons so that he could take over the galaxy. The goal of the game's heroes was to destroy the villain's weapons before Dedstorm could activate them. The action took place on a large imaginary landscape.

Multiple players with different attributes on a large, varied playing field, Tom thought. Galaxy Masters would be a huge programming challenge, but a lot of fun to try.

But what Tom said was "Forget it. I'm not programming the TRG for a role-playing game."

"So you *could* do it!" Alan said.

"It would take a long time," Tom pointed out.

"We have time," Alan said excitedly. "The whole team could help." Tom's teammates, besides Alan, were Mandy Coster, Rick Cantwell, and Maria Santana.

16

"If we lose tomorrow," Alan went on, "we'll be tied with Gary Gitmoe's team with one loss each. Then we'd have to play them again Monday. We could program over the weekend."

Tom considered this. Gary Gitmoe played the role of Dedstorm for the other top team in the tournament. Gary and his friends had lost only once, in an earlier round. It was Gary's team that Tom's group would have to face for the double-elimination championship.

"It's just not right for the TRG," Tom said. "And I don't think we'll lose tomorrow."

"Don't be too sure," Alan told him. "Anyway, we'll talk about it later. I want to get back to drilling."

"Are you sure you're feeling okay?"

"Terrific! Come on, Tom. Get me back down there."

Tom hesitated before lowering the helmet. "Okay," he said to Alan. "But this time while you're in the simulation, I want you to check out the heads-up display."

"The what?"

"A heads-up display like the ones fighter pilots use. You'll see information projected into the air in front of you, but you'll have to look in just the right place."

The helmet now covered Alan's head again. "Just keep in mind while you're drilling that this is all a simulation, okay?"

"Right, right," Alan said impatiently. His hand found the control switch, and he flipped it.

Immediately a warning bell sounded, and Alan's body went rigid.

"Alan?" Tom said, grasping his friend's arm. "Alan? Are you okay?"

No answer.

Then, as Tom watched in growing horror, his friend's muscles jerked in sudden, violent spasms.

3

THERE WAS NO DOUBT IN TOM'S MIND. ALAN'S BODY had suffered the painful jolt of electrocution. Using as much strength as he dared, Tom tried to pry his friend's fingers free to get at the switch, but Alan's grip on the armrest was like steel.

With the warning bell screaming in his ears, Tom dashed to the control room. There on the screens, at ten times normal speed, Tom could see Alan operating his drill. Good. Tom sighed with relief. Alan was conscious.

Then glancing through the glass wall, Tom saw that Alan was no longer rigidly gripping the armrest—another good sign.

Tom switched the TRG to normal speed and turned on his mike. The screen showed Alan frantically pulling levers.

19

"Alan, are you okay?"

"Tom!" Alan's image trembled as a simulated earthquake shook the sub. "You don't know how glad I am to hear you!" There was genuine panic in Alan's voice. "I've stopped drilling, but these tremors keep getting stronger, anyway!"

"Hey, relax," Tom said. "You can bail out anytime if it gets too intense."

"I'm trying to bail out! I can't disengage the drill!"

On the monitor Tom saw the strain on Alan's face. Suddenly Tom realized what was happening.

Alan was no longer aware that he was in the simulator!

Tom reached over to the heads-up display controls and typed something in. Then he said, "Alan, look up."

Alan raised his head. His eyes were wild with fear.

"No, I mean raise your eyes. Look at your eyebrows."

Alan pounded on the control panel. "How's that going to help?" Tom remembered how he'd struggled to contain his own panic, and he had been fully aware that he was in a simulation.

"Trust me," Tom said, keeping his voice calm. "Roll your eyes up."

Finally Alan did as he was told.

" 'This is a simulation of the Total Reality Generator,' " Alan read aloud. Some of the panic left his voice. Then another tremor hit the sub, and Alan cried, "No way! This is real!"

"Hang on, Alan. Just hang on." Tom pressed the Simulation Over button, and the screens showing Alan's world turned to electronic snow.

Minutes later Alan and Tom were sprawled on the ground-level roof of Tom's bunker, looking out at the buildings of Swift Enterprises.

"Weird," Alan said. He propped himself up on one elbow. "I really thought I was running the DIVE in a drilling experiment. I forgot all about the TRG."

"You got hit by a small power surge," Tom explained. "The warning bell went off right after the simulation started."

"A power surge?"

"One of Megatron's jobs is to regulate the flow of electricity to various parts of the Swift Enterprise power grid. If Megatron sends too much power, there's a surge. This time the energy pulse was weak—I have safeguards built into the TRG— but it did knock you out. When you came to, you thought the simulation was real." Tom peered closely at his friend, who was still pale. "Are you sure you're okay?"

"I'm fine." Alan checked his watch, then jumped up. "But I won't be for long if I miss dinner again. We're having curried vegetables with hot and sour fish. My dad's cooking. Hey, want to join us?"

"On one condition," Tom said, getting to his feet.

"Which is?"

"That you drop this idea of using the TRG to play Galaxy Masters."

"Consider it dropped," Alan said, raising his hands in surrender, "even if it *is* a terrific idea."

Tom realized that programming the TRG for Galaxy Masters *was* a terrific idea, if only he could solve the power surge problem. He couldn't stop thinking about Alan's suggestion after school the next day as his team squared off against Dedstorm, played by Gary Gitmoe, in the Jefferson High computer lab. In the first half of the game, Alan, playing the evil Dedstorm against Gary's team of heroes, had lost. The heroes on Gary's squad had made their way to the City of the Ancients, inserted their memory cube into the arsenal guardhouse, and destroyed Dedstorm's drone army. Now if Gary defeated Tom's team of heroes, Gitmoe's team would win the first round of the double elimination.

Tom saw that the small computer lab was crowded with spectators—mostly players from defeated teams. Gary's team of Tracy Shaw, Jessica Trine, Bob Wolf, and Dan Coster crowded around the game table, watching Gary maneuver Dedstorm against Tom's crew.

Most role-playing games didn't use a computer, but Galaxy Masters used two: one for the game referee, and one for the player who took the role of the villainous Dedstorm. The computers were linked so that Dedstorm could enter his moves in secret.

It was late in the game, and Gary Gitmoe was making good use of his secret moves. Tom and his friends announced their moves to Les Hempel. As co-designer, Les had been a logical choice to referee the game. Les then keyed the information into his computer. Meanwhile, Gary just smiled and typed in Dedstorm's moves. The spectators were silent, busy visualizing the game. Following the action was a little like listening to a story told aloud.

"It's not fair," Mandy Coster said. She had the role of Princess Nirvana on Tom's team. "Not only is my character imprisoned, but Dedstorm gets to make moves in secret, and we don't!"

"Moving in secret didn't help Alan win, did it?" her cousin, Dan Coster, taunted her.

"Speaking of imprisoned characters," said Maria Santana, who was playing the role of the wizard Chameleon, "I'm still trying to escape from this cage of Dedstorm's."

"How are you trying to get out?" Les asked.

Maria frowned, running her fingers thoughtfully through her black curls. "How about making grass grow up and cover the cage's energy emitters?"

"Won't work," Gary Gitmoe said. "It's a stupid move."

"Hey, Gary," said Tracy Shaw, Gary's team-mate, "that was uncalled for."

"Dedstorm has no manners," Gary sneered. "Ruthlessness is what makes him strong."

"I think this game is going to your head," Tracy retorted.

"Anyway, grass won't grow in the City of the

Ancients," Les told Maria. "There's no soil. You're still imprisoned. And as for Mandy's—I mean, Princess Nirvana's—complaint, your moves aren't secret because Dedstorm's deathhawk is spying on you and can hear everything you say."

Tom frowned in concentration, visualizing the game situation. "Dedstorm's power supply is almost unlimited."

"*Almost* is the key word," Les said. "But Dedstorm can be worn down, as your team has proven against other opponents."

"Those other teams played Dedstorm like a wimp," Gary Gitmoe said with a grin. He entered his next move.

Les read the move on his screen and announced, "Dedstorm has just attacked what's left of your team with six energy wraiths and three cyborgs, who were hiding in the bushes."

"I think this game is coming to a close." Gary leaned back in his seat and crossed his arms on his chest in a satisfied manner.

"Ha!" said Rick Cantwell. He was the only member of Tom's team that Gary had not successfully isolated from Tom's character, Tinker. Rick played the role of the Denebian envoy, a giant, blue-skinned alien. "The envoy eats energy wraiths for dinner," Rick said with a grin. "And speaking of dinner, I'm starved. Let's hurry up and win, Tom— I mean, Tinker—so we can get some pizza."

Gary continued to enter his moves.

"While the envoy is talking about pizza," Les said, never taking his eyes from the computer screen, "two cyborgs tackle him and the third lands a blow on his head. The envoy is knocked down and should be dazed. All six wraiths are coming after Tinker."

"Hey!" Rick cried. "The envoy never had trouble with cyborgs before!"

"He never had three attack him at once," Les said.

Dan Coster, who was standing behind Les, squinted at the screen. "How can you tell what's going on? All I see are some dots and boxes full of numbers."

"The computer is just an aid for the game referee," Les told him. "Using fancy graphics would be a waste of programming, since the game is played in the players' imaginations. I just need the dots to tell me where the characters are on the map and what their condition is."

Les pointed at the screen. "See that flashing number? That's the envoy's consciousness index. That's how I know that the cyborgs have almost knocked him out." Les turned to Tom. "So what's your move, Tinker?"

Tom looked down at his hands, trying to imagine Tinker's equipment. This was where training with the TRG would have really helped.

Let's see, Tom thought. Tinker has his bag of tools, a spool of copper wire, some rope, and his main weapon, the puzzle gun. The frame of the puzzle gun looked like a chrome machine gun, but its single chamber could hold three glowing crystal cylinders. The cylinders altered the energy that flowed through them from the gun. Green arrows ran along the sides of the cylinders, showing the direction of energy flow.

Tom knew he was taking too long.

Les said, "The first wraith grabs your shoulder. Heat sizzles through your tinker's vest."

"I jump back," Tom said.

"Another wraith reaches for you."

"I dodge," Tom responded quickly. "I keep dodging, and I'm rearranging the elements of the puzzle gun."

"Better hurry," Les warned him.

"I'm kicking the cyborgs," Rick said.

"But you're dazed," Les said. "You aren't kicking hard enough. A cyborg hits your head and you're out cold."

Rick slapped his thigh in frustration. "Stupid cyborgs."

"Way to go, Gary!" cheered Bob Wolf, who was the Denebian envoy for Gary's team. He smiled at his girlfriend, Jessica, who played Chameleon, the team's wizard. "The game will be over in time for us to catch some waves."

"Is surfing all you ever think about?" Jessica teased him.

Tom, still trying to visualize Tinker's equipment, said, "I'll use the Amplify, Focus, and Radiate cylinders." He imagined himself sliding the glowing elements into the puzzle gun like exotic batteries.

Les entered the move.

"As soon as I have it assembled," Tom went on, "I aim the puzzle gun at the nearest wraith and fire."

"Zap!" Mandy cheered. Maria added, "Fried wraith!"

"Yes," Les said. "With that assembly, the puzzle gun works as a particle weapon. The wraith is vaporized."

Gary Gitmoe typed something into his terminal.

"I'm zapping the second wraith," Tom said.

"Nothing's left but smoking footprints," Les reported.

Gary finished typing in his move.

"I fire at a third one," Tom said.

"Zap. Three wraiths destroyed. However," Les said, peering over his screen to look at Tom, "while you were distracted, the cyborgs stole the second memory cube from the Denebian envoy. They gave it to one of the remaining wraiths. All three wraiths are now streaking skyward."

"Hey!" Rick protested.

"You're unconscious, Envoy," Les reminded him.

"I fire at the escaping wraiths," Tom said.

"They're already quite far away." Les checked the computer. "But you do hit one. Not the one with the cube, though."

"I fire again."

"They're out of range."

"Then Tinker is going to chase the wraiths," Tom said, thinking quickly. "I'm reassembling the puzzle gun to make . . ." What were all seven of the elements of the puzzle gun? Again he tried to see them in his mind's eye.

"Better hurry," Les warned. Gary was tapping another move into the computer.

"I'm making an energized vaulting pole by loading the puzzle gun with cylinders for Amplify, Focus, and Repel."

"Before you finish, the ground next to you explodes in a flash of light," Les reported. "You look up and see Dedstorm's deathhawk preparing to fire another blast."

Gary laughed. "Prepare to die, Tinker."

"I change the last cylinder from Repel to Radiate," Tom said, "and shoot at the deathhawk."

Les tapped the computer keys, then said, "The deathhawk is a small target. You missed. And Dedstorm has distracted you long enough for his wraiths to get away with the cube."

"Oh, no," Mandy groaned. In her brown eyes, Tom saw a trace of real disappointment. "Now Dedstorm has both memory cubes! He can activate the sleeping army of the Ancients!"

"And I'll use that army to divide and conquer the galaxy," Gary said, "just like I divided and conquered your team, Tom Swift. Game over." And then, savoring the words, he added, "You lose."

Les nodded. "Dedstorm wins."

The spectators burst into cheers.

"Good game, anyway," someone said, slapping Tom's back.

"At least we can grab that pizza now," Rick said.

"Can't win them all." Tom shrugged. "Congratulations, Gary. You played a good game." He reached across the table to shake hands.

"Save that good sport stuff for somebody else," Gary said, ignoring Tom's hand. "I creamed you."

"Gary!" Tracy Shaw glared at her teammate, but Gary ignored her.

"All right!" said Dan Coster, trading a high five with Gary. "Our team rules!"

"Oh, be quiet, Dan," Mandy told him. "I still can't believe you'd play on a team against us."

"Hey, cousin," Dan said, "I'm just better than you are at picking a winner." Then he added, "Sorry, Tom-Tom, but nice guys finish last. Gary takes no prisoners."

"No one is champion yet," Les reminded him. "Gary's team lost once in an earlier round, and this is the first defeat for Tom's team. Monday's winner will be the champion."

"What if we split?" Dan asked. "I mean, who wins if Alan beats our heroes and Gary beats theirs?"

"Your team swept the rounds today, so you'd win."

"Sweet!" Dan said.

"We're running out of room here in the computer lab," Les went on, "so the final game will be in the school cafeteria. My dad will provide the computers for simultaneous play. Everyone's welcome to watch."

"That's right," Gary said. "The whole school can show up to see Tom and his friends get totally humiliated."

"Hey," Rick said, shoving back his chair and

standing up. "Haven't you ever heard of winning graciously?"

"Weaklings win graciously," Gary shot back, "because sooner or later they're going to lose. The strong get what they deserve. So do the weak."

"Tell it like it is!" Dan yelled.

Rick set his jaw. As quarterback for Jefferson High's football team, he was used to the ups and downs of sometimes winning, sometimes losing. But Gary challenged more than Rick's sense of fair play.

"You're talking like some kind of dictator." Rick spat out the words.

"And you're talking like a coward," Gary answered.

Rick leaned forward. Tom caught one of his arms, and Alan grabbed the other. "Come on, Rick," Tom said. "It's only a game."

"So is football," Rick said in an angry tone. "But how you play it says a lot about what kind of person you are."

"Well, this is encouraging," said an unfamiliar voice.

Everyone turned to face the man in the doorway. His black hair was streaked with gray at the temples.

"Hi, Dad," Les said.

Mr. Hempel smiled. "This must be a pretty good game that Les and I designed, if you're willing to start a fight over it." He stepped into the room, extending his hand toward Tom. "You must be

Tom Swift. I worked on a project once with your father."

"Hi," Tom said as he shook hands. "You aren't exactly meeting us at our best, Mr. Hempel."

"Oh, I understand completely," Les's father replied. "Spirit of competition and all that." He turned to Rick. "But it's not really worth fighting about, is it?"

Rick shook his shoulders, and Tom and Alan let go of him. "There's more to it than that," Rick said quietly.

With the tension broken, the room began to empty.

"I think I'll help referee the deciding game of your tournament," Mr. Hempel said. "That way I can see if Galaxy Masters is ready to be marketed."

"Our team will be there," Rick said, glaring at Gary.

"So will mine," Gary said, glaring back. "And I'll win."

"Come on," Tom said, grabbing Rick's elbow. "We were going for pizza, remember?"

Rick turned away from Gary Gitmoe. "How could I forget? Nice meeting you, Mr. Hempel."

After Tom's team had stepped into the hallway, Maria asked, "Why is Gary being such a poor sport?"

"Being a good sport means having a decent thought about your opponent," Rick told her. "I'm not kidding when I say Gary sounds like a dictator. That's a poisonous philosophy, that stuff about the weak and the strong."

Mandy nodded. "I'm worried about the effect Gary is having on Dan. He's actually buying into that stuff."

"Remember," Tom said, "it's only a game."

"No, Tom, it's more than that," Mandy said. "My cousin's an impressionable kind of guy. What if playing this game Gary's way makes him believe that might really does make right?"

"It's not just Dan," Rick put in. "Everybody who watches could get the idea that it pays to be ruthless. A game like this is more than a game, Tom. It's a clash of philosophies. Gary is trashing everything I stand for. And I know that you feel the same way."

"I hear you," Tom said. "You're right. It's not just another game. We have to beat Gary on Monday."

Alan had been silent until then. Now he said softly, "I don't know if we can."

"Sure we can," Tom said.

"No," Alan said more firmly. "I agree that there's more at stake here than just a game. But I've been watching Gary's strategy for a few games now, and there's something you all should know."

Alan halted, and the others stopped and looked at him.

"Galaxy Masters is a flawed game. Gary is going to cream us on Monday, just as he says."

4

THE NEXT DAY WAS SATURDAY, AND MANY OF THE students from Jefferson High were enjoying the sun and sea at Laguna Pequeña beach. Dan Coster's band, the Scavengers, was playing some original tunes, powering their electric guitars with a portable generator. Tom sat on a beach towel, lost in thought as he watched surfers negotiate the waves. He tapped his fingers in time with the band's drummer: *Kata-thump, kata-thump, kata-kata-kata-thump.*

"Hi, genius," said Mandy Coster as she and Tom's sister, Sandra, spread their beach towels near Tom's. Mandy was wearing a red swimsuit, and her long chestnut hair blew in the breeze. "You look like you're thinking about Galaxy Masters."

"Sort of," Tom said. Actually, he was wrestling with Megatron's power surge problem. If he could solve that puzzle, then he could safely use the TRG to find a winning strategy for Galaxy Masters.

A Frisbee landed in the sand between Tom and Sandra, and Rick and Alan came running up, racing each other to the disk. Alan reached for it, but Rick tackled him. They crashed to the ground, sending a spray of sand in the girls' direction.

"Hey, you guys!" Sandra yelled. "Are you trying to bury us alive?"

"Sorry." Grinning, Rick scrambled to his feet with the Frisbee raised high. "Victory!" Then he said, "Speaking of victory, do you guys want to talk about Galaxy Masters? We've got practically our whole team here."

"Except for Maria," Mandy said. "She had to work at her parents' greenhouse today."

"How about it, Tom," Rick said. "Have you figured out how to beat Gary yet? Alan isn't right, is he?"

Tom smiled reassuringly. "There shouldn't be such a thing as an unbeatable strategy," he said. "Gary's approach has to have a flaw."

"Unless I'm right and the game is truly flawed," Alan said, moving to sit cross-legged in the sand. "I'm so sure that Gary's strategy is unbeatable that, as Dedstorm, I'm going to use it against Gary's own team. I'll either separate Tinker's forces or make Tinker use up his puzzle gun energy to keep them together. Either way, Tinker has to lose."

34

"There must be something Tinker can do," Tom said. But deep down, he was beginning to have his doubts. Maybe Alan was right. Les and his father wouldn't deliberately write the game to be uneven, but Galaxy Masters was still in the testing stage. It could be flawed.

"I know I promised not to mention something"—Alan leaned closer to Tom—"so I won't mention it. But I think you ought to think about it, anyway. It might help us out."

"What's he talking about?" Mandy asked.

Before Tom could answer, Dan Coster's band suddenly stopped playing in the middle of a tune. Tom looked over at the makeshift bandstand. Dan seemed to be having an argument with a guy who was carrying a guitar.

Sandra turned to look, too. "Who is that?" she asked.

"Ed Griffy," Rick said. "He's Dan's rhythm guitarist, but he hasn't played with the band for a while. He had his hand in a cast for a long time. Now, what's that mysterious something that Alan is talking about?"

"Well," Tom said, "I have this new invention. It's a simulator that I call a Total Reality Generator. Actually, the name is ahead of the technology. The artificial reality isn't quite perfect."

"I'm sure there are some things that just can't be simulated," Mandy said.

"Like what?" Rick asked. Mandy looked at Tom and blushed. Rick grinned and nudged her.

"Anyway," Tom went on, "Alan wanted me to

program the TRG for Galaxy Masters. I might learn something helpful."

"Sounds great!" Rick said. "Why not go for it?"

"I know why," Sandra said. "It has to do with the fuzzy logic circuits, doesn't it, Tom?"

Tom nodded. "The TRG can't work without those circuits, but putting them into Megatron has had some unexpected results."

"Like causing power surges," Sandra told the others. "Lately the supercomputer doesn't regulate electricity flow as well as it should. And Dad isn't exactly happy about that."

"Dad's been putting up with the problem because he believes in the TRG," Tom said. "He knows that I'm doing my best to work out the bugs, but I haven't made much progress. The Megatron supercomputer designed its own fuzzy logic circuits. We're still trying to understand how they work."

"I still say go for it," Rick said. "Anything to beat Gary Gitmoe."

"It may be our only chance, Tom," Alan said. "I'll help you do the programming."

As Tom looked out at the waves again, Sandra said, "Uh-oh. He's getting that look in his eyes."

"Well, running a complex scenario like Galaxy Masters has certain advantages over testing the equipment with a deep-drilling program."

The others were silent as Tom continued to think out loud. "I guess I can justify it as part of the overall testing. But it'll take a while to program. We'd have to feed the rule book into Megatron and explain what's happened in every game so far. That could take all weekend."

"What are we waiting for?" Mandy said, picking up her beach towel. "Next stop, Swift Enterprises."

Rick and Alan said, "All right!"

Mandy and Sandra gathered up their beach gear, and then they all started toward the parking lot. As they passed the band they heard Dan shouting at Ed Griffy. "I don't care if your hand was in a cast. You don't make practice, you're out of the Scavengers. I have a replacement rhythm guitar."

"We've got room for another guitar," the new guitarist called out.

Dan whirled on him. "It's my band," he yelled, jabbing his finger in the new guitarist's direction. "I make the rules. Ed is history. He's got to learn something about the way the world works. Sob stories don't get you anywhere."

"Can you believe your cousin?" Sandra shook her head.

"He sounds like Gary Gitmoe," Mandy said sadly as she and Sandra piled into Alan's car. Tom went with Rick in his friend's classic sports car.

As they pulled out of the lot and headed for Swift Enterprises, Rick said, "I wish we'd just get this game over with. The whole thing is getting under my skin." Rick drove slowly on the highway, Tom noticed, which was out of character for Central Hill's notorious speed demon. Suddenly Tom realized why.

"And *I* wish," Tom said, "that you would finally

tune this car. Your engine sounds more like a can full of gravel than a well-made machine. Want me to help you get it into shape?"

Rick patted the dashboard of his fifteen-year-old red Jaguar XKE. "Nobody works on this precious baby but me."

"Which means"—Tom laughed—"that nobody works on it, period."

Rick shrugged. "What can I say? I'm a busy guy."

After they had passed through the Swift Enterprises security gate, they parked next to Alan's car. Sandra, Alan, and Mandy were already waiting to see the Total Reality Generator.

Tom led them down to his lab. He pressed his palm to the handprint recognition panel on the wall, and they passed through the first door. At the second door, a voice asked, "Which guitar-playing sisters have a lot of Heart?"

"Ann and Nancy Wilson," Tom said, and the door opened.

"I knew that one," Mandy said.

"But the door wouldn't have opened for you," Rick told her. "The door recognizes Tom's voice pattern." Then, in a conspiratorial whisper, he added, "It doesn't really matter whether he gets the rock trivia right."

"Not that I'd be likely to get it wrong," Tom said over his shoulder, "since I wrote all the questions myself."

Tom stepped into the lab with the others right behind him.

"Wow." Rick gazed at the oversize helmet and the leather-and-chrome chair. "Some of your inventions have looked cool, Tom, but this one takes the prize. It looks like something from the bridge of a starship."

"Well, that's a possibility," Tom said. "When I finish developing it, the TRG will be able to simulate any machine or experience. You'll be able to use it to earn a pilot's license, learn to play the piano, or improve your batting average. Or command a starship."

"Can we try it out?" Mandy asked.

Tom gazed at the control panel. He hated to say no to his friends, but he couldn't take a chance that they might get hurt by a power surge. Still, a new circuit breaker could provide fail-safe protection. "Maybe later," he said. "Right now we'd better get started with the programming." He went into the control room and quickly set up a microphone and headset for each of his friends.

"Alan and I will work on the main programming," he said. "As we feed in information on the game rules and Gary's strategy, Megatron will ask the rest of you questions, to fill in the background details. Tell the computer whatever it needs to know."

"But I haven't played the game," Sandra said.

"You've watched, though," Tom told her. He turned to Alan. "Do you have the game rules?"

Alan held up the Galaxy Masters handbook. "I've been carrying this around all day," he said, "looking for a way to beat Gary."

"All right," Tom said. "Let's get to work. This is a lot for Megatron to take in. It may take a while."

Tom was right—it took most of the weekend. Rick and Sandra answered Megatron's questions the rest of that Saturday, and Maria Santana helped when she had a few free hours on Sunday morning. Tom and Alan handled the formal programming, sitting at the control-room consoles.

"Megatron sure asks some funny questions," Sandra told Tom on Sunday afternoon.

"It sure does," Rick agreed. "Just now it asked me to verify that Dan Coster and Mandy are cousins, and then it wanted to know the name of Dan's band."

"And what does Rick's stomach have to do with Galaxy Masters?" Sandra asked. "When I mentioned that Rick kept thinking about pizza during the last game, Megatron asked how many grams of protein Rick consumes in a day."

Alan and Tom looked at each other and shrugged.

Tom brought Megatron's voice reader on-line at his programming station. "Megatron?"

"Ready," said the mechanical voice.

"Query," Tom said. "Why do you require personal information on Dan and Mandy Coster and on Rick?"

"Understood," Megatron said. After a pause, the computer answered. "In the Galaxy Masters game, as in all role-playing games, the personalities of the players strongly influence the game events. To simulate the game, I must have access to personality traits."

"But we want to simulate the play of our team against Gary Gitmoe's strategy," Tom told Megatron. "Dan Coster plays the role of Tinker for Gary's team, so he won't figure in the scenario we want you to simulate."

"In order to achieve Total Reality Generation," Megatron said, "ancillary data is required. Game rules supply insufficient information. I'm also accessing the security files."

"What does that mean?" Rick asked, a puzzled look on his face.

"Basically," Tom said, "it's Megatron's way of saying 'Trust me.' " Into his console mike, he said, "Megatron, this won't change the basic nature of the game, will it?"

"Negative," the machine responded. "All essential elements of strategy remain intact. Ancillary data will make for more psychologically satisfying play."

"What information from the security files would Megatron need?" Sandra wondered.

Tom asked the computer and was chilled by the two-word reply: "Xavier Mace."

"The Black Dragon," Tom said, his voice almost a whisper. More than once, Tom had tangled with Mace. The man was brilliant, and pure evil.

"Dedstorm is described by the Galaxy Masters rules as an archfiend," Megatron said. "By cross-referencing my files, I found Xavier Mace to be the closest psychological match. For the simulation,

Dedstorm will express the ruthless personality of the Black Dragon."

"Well," Tom told his friends, not sure that he liked this development, "at least Megatron is aiming for authenticity. Go ahead and answer his questions."

Rick and Sandra did so until they were hoarse.

Hours later only Tom and Alan remained in the lab. They were discussing what the program still needed, when they were interrupted by Megatron.

"Information processing is now complete," said the computer's synthesized voice. "Simulation is ready to run."

Alan looked at Tom. "How's that possible?" he said. "There's a lot that we still haven't programmed in."

"Fuzzy logic," Tom said. "With those new logic circuits, Megatron can make educated guesses about things we haven't yet mentioned."

"So the Galaxy Masters simulation is actually ready?"

"As soon as I make one hardware adjustment," Tom said, opening a control panel. "I'm going to add a circuit breaker so any power surge will end the simulation. No more surprises like yesterday."

But before Tom could get to work, a horn sounded over the lab's speaker systems.

"Security alert! Security alert!" boomed an amplified voice. "Class Two security alert. Fire, with injuries, in building fifteen!"

5

SECURITY ALERT!" THE SPEAKER BLASTED AGAIN. "Fire in building fifteen! Damage control personnel report at once!"

"Building fifteen," Tom said, letting the control panel snap shut. "That's where Dad's working on supercompacted electric batteries. Come on, Alan!"

Tom and Alan raced out of the lab. In the corridor, they were almost bowled over by a white-haired man in uniform—Harlan Ames, chief of security for Swift Enterprises.

"Harlan," Tom said, "can you fill us in?"

"Power surge," the security chief replied without breaking stride. "Apparently a couple of technicians were zapped by the electrical discharge, but they weren't seriously hurt."

"And the fire?" Tom asked, jogging close on Harlan's heels.

"It must have started when a transformer blew." The older man's tanned face creased with a frown as he shoved open the outside doors. "I can't say I'm happy about all these power glitches that Megatron is causing lately."

Plunging into the bright California sunlight, Tom saw smoke rising from building fifteen's vents.

Tom and Alan dashed after the security chief, into the building and up a flight of stairs, then into a lab. What they saw made Alan's jaw drop. In the center of the room was a large, messy pile of square ceramic wafers, each the size of a compact disk box. Glittering blue sparks arced and jumped from wafer to wafer like tiny lightning bolts.

"Wow!" Alan exclaimed. "What are those?"

"Experimental batteries," Tom said. "They work with solid electricity. Each one, when they're perfected, will store as much power as thirty standard car batteries."

As Tom spoke, his father and several assistants rushed to place a containment barrier around the sparking equipment. Off in a corner of the room, a blown transformer—coated with a white firefighting powder—was still smoking.

"What's with the plastic sheeting?" Alan moved closer.

Tom raised an arm to keep him back. "The containment barrier may look like ordinary plastic," he told him, "but it's really the product of sophisticated electronics. Watch what happens as the barrier comes closer to the batteries."

When the pile sent tiny lightning bolts leaping toward Mr. Swift and his assistants, Tom and Alan could see that the discharges were absorbed by the sheet. The barrier rippled, changed shape, and drew the discharge to different sections so that no part was overloaded.

As thin as it was, the sheet was obviously quite heavy. The technicians and security people struggled to maneuver it.

"Let's give them a hand," Tom said, stepping forward.

"Careful," Mr. Swift warned. His piercing blue eyes darted from the pile of sizzling batteries to the barrier. Mr. Swift's blond hair was streaked with gray, but he still had much of his son's youthful intensity.

"Bring it in," Mr. Swift said, "but don't raise the barrier up from the floor. If you do—"

"Alan, watch it!" Tom shouted. In trying to muscle the barrier into place, Alan had accidentally raised it a fraction of an inch from the floor.

A bright flash shot across the room. As Tom watched, Alan sat down hard on the concrete floor, then looked with astonishment at the smoking soles of his shoes.

Tom and his father were at Alan's side in a second. "Are you okay?" Tom asked.

Alan nodded, looking bewildered. "Yeah, fine. Just a little surprised."

"That was just the sort of discharge jolt I'm trying to prevent with the barrier," Mr. Swift said. "The barrier will let the batteries drain in a controlled manner. Then we can restack them into a stable configuration. Are you sure you're all right?"

Harlan Ames knelt next to Alan. "We'd better take him to the infirmary to get checked out, just in case."

Mr. Swift agreed, and Tom said, "I'll go with him."

"You can follow in a minute," his father said. "Right now, I need your assistance."

Alan started to his feet, but Harlan Ames made him wait to be carried to the medical van. "We don't want you walking if the soles of your feet have been burned."

"I'm fine," Alan protested, but the head of security insisted on taking every possible precaution.

After two Swift Enterprises security guards had carried Alan from the room, Mr. Swift motioned Tom toward one of Megatron's consoles, mounted in the wall.

"Megatron," Mr. Swift said, "please analyze the source of this fire."

"This fire originated with the overload and explosion of transformer unit 0677. That unit is now inoperative," said the computer's voice.

"Yes," Mr. Swift said, "it's thoroughly destroyed. Tell me, Megatron: Why did the unit overload?"

"There was a surge in power delivered to the unit."

"Why?"

Megatron paused for a moment. "Records show that my power delivery program malfunctioned."

"And why was that?"

"Power demand increased slightly, and I over-corrected. The fault appears to lie in my new fuzzy logic circuits. Further analysis is not possible at this time."

"Just what is this fuzzy logic business about?" asked Harlan Ames, who had returned in time to hear the computer's explanation.

"It's a new computer logic," Tom said. "Computers have always been programmed in binary code, like yes and no, with no in-between state. But with fuzzy logic, Megatron can think in terms of 'maybe.' It gives Megatron the power to have a hunch about things it doesn't absolutely know."

Harlan Ames waved his hand. "This is beyond me," he said, "but I do know that if we keep having surges like this, sooner or later someone's going to be seriously hurt."

"True." Mr. Swift turned toward his son. "Tom," he said, "this was an expensive malfunction."

Tom looked around the room. "I can see that."

"More important, Harlan is right. The technicians and Alan seem to be okay, but what about next time?"

The batteries had now been surrounded by the

containment barrier, and their blue glitter was dimming.

"I'm all for testing new technology," Mr. Swift said. "At the same time, Tom, I'm starting to think that you should pull Megatron's fuzzy logic circuits. At least until we have a better fix on why they're causing problems."

Tom frowned. "Dad, the Total Reality Generator isn't just an interesting experiment. It's going to save lives. I've already programmed it to train deep-sea drill operators. But the TRG can't run without fuzzy logic."

The transformer shot out one last puff of smoke.

"As long as we know that power surges are possible," Tom said, "we can protect ourselves against them. I'm putting a cutout circuit into the TRG, for instance. And by leaving the fuzzy logic circuits in place, we can figure out what the problem is. Unexpected glitches might reveal what we need to know to fix the circuits."

Mr. Swift scratched his head. "Megatron," he said, "how likely is another serious surge in the next two days?"

"Probability of less than one tenth of one percent," said Megatron. "However, the chance of one or more milder surges is almost one hundred percent. Those milder surges should cause no damage to equipment."

"All right," Mr. Swift said. "I can deal with one tenth of one percent. But, Tom, you'd better figure out what's going on, or we won't have any alterna-

tive to pulling those circuits. You've got two
days."

"Two days," Alan said, opening the infirmary
door marked Exit. "It's nail-biting time, dude. And
you're not going to have a lot of free hours to
work, what with school and then the championship tomorrow." As they stepped out into the late-
night air, he looked at Tom uncertainly. "You're
still going to play, aren't you?"

"Hey," Tom said, "would I let my friends
down?"

Alan smiled and visibly relaxed. "No, I don't
suppose you would."

"How are your feet?"

"Fine," Alan said. He lifted one shoe so that the
charred sole showed. "My shoes are pretty much
toasted, though."

"Casualties in the march of progress," Tom
joked. Inwardly, though, Tom blamed himself for
putting Alan in harm's way. "Dad will replace
them, if you want."

"Great," Alan said. Then he looked thoughtful.
"Tom, how *are* you going to work on the fuzzy
logic problem?"

"I'll get it done," Tom said, trying to reassure
himself as much as Alan. He had his doubts about
meeting his father's deadline. Finding out why
Megatron was malfunctioning was important. So
was winning the game. Rick and Mandy had convinced him that more was at stake than the tournament itself, and he had promised them that

they'd win. But he had no idea how, and the uncertainty was beginning to wear on him.

Hours later, Tom lay in bed, staring at the ceiling. He kept turning over in his mind the Galaxy Masters rules, then everything he knew about Megatron's new circuits. What sort of bug would cause Megatron to malfunction? Megatron was having a hard time with what had once been routine tasks.

Something else nagged at the back of Tom's mind. There was something he had left undone.

Tom sat up in bed. He and Alan had left the TRG powered up and ready to run. He quickly dressed, intending to go to the lab and turn the TRG off. It was past midnight. This was hardly the time to test the role-playing program. He'd just have to trust his wits when it came to the next day's game.

Once he was inside the lab, though, Tom was drawn to the TRG, its shining black helmet seeming to beckon.

What could it hurt, he thought, to run just a quick simulation? The more he knew about his invention, the more he might discover about the fuzzy logic circuits. And maybe a quick test would give him the edge he needed for tomorrow's game.

"Megatron," Tom said, climbing into the chair, "prepare to run the Galaxy Masters simulation."

"The simulation has been ready to run since this afternoon," Megatron answered. "I'm still standing by."

"Okay," Tom said. He glanced at the control room. There really should have been someone to oversee the simulation. But he'd make it a short run—quick and safe. "Let's do it." He lowered the helmet.

"Do you wish to play the role of Tinker?"

"Yes," Tom said. "Just as I will tomorrow."

For a moment Tom could feel the tingle of the electrodes making contact with his scalp.

"Where shall I start the scenario?" Megatron asked.

"Let's try it from halfway through the game," Tom said. "That's where my team began to have problems with Gary Gitmoe."

"Understood," Megatron said.

The air around Tom seemed to fill with the snow of video static, and he heard the gentle hiss of white noise.

Megatron said, "Starting simulation—"

The next thing Tom should have heard was the word "now" from Megatron. Instead, he heard the lab's warning bell and felt a sharp jolt from the helmet. Only partly aware of what was happening, Tom felt his body go rigid with electric shock.

Then he blacked out.

6

"TINKER! ARE YOU ALL RIGHT?" SOMEONE WAS pulling on his arm. "Tinker?"

His eyes flew open, and he half sat up. The person—the *creature*—who was yanking his arm had bluish skin and was huge. Stars twinkled behind the giant's shoulders, and in another part of the sky the moon shone brightly.

He closed his eyes and sank back onto the ground again. Some weird dream! But the dream wouldn't quit. The huge hand kept shaking him.

"He just about took your head off!" said the giant.

"Where am I?" For that matter, he thought, *who am I?*

"Scrambled your brains, he did. He hit you with this, but I made sure he left it behind." The giant waved something in the air: a silvery arm. Tinker stared at the arm in confusion. What was going on? With the giant's help, he rose to his feet.

"Come on!" the giant urged. "We've got to keep moving!" He threw the metal arm aside and pointed at something on the ground. "Get that pack onto your shoulders again, and let's go before—"

A stab of light bolted from the sky, and the ground near their feet exploded in a sizzle of electricity. Instinctively Tinker rolled away from the blast.

"Too late! Run!" shouted the blue giant, picking up the leather pack and slinging it onto his shoulder. He was already carrying a pack of his own, a huge one.

Tinker didn't need to be told twice. He sprinted forward. Whatever was going on, the giant seemed to be his friend, and the two of them were under fire.

"Take cover!" the giant yelled.

Tinker dived behind a rock just as the ground where he had been a moment before exploded. There was silence, then the whir of metallic wings. Tinker sat up, then ducked just in time as something razor sharp sliced through the air near his face. As it passed, Tinker caught a quick glimpse of a hawk, its talons extended. The mechanical bird turned a malevolent eye on Tinker.

"Get out of here, you silicon-brained vulture!" yelled the giant, throwing a rock at the bird. Then he turned to Tinker. "The deathhawk isn't usually so bold. Must have figured out you were shaken up. But we'll have a moment's peace now. It'll take the deathhawk a while to recharge."

A blue hand reached down to pull Tinker to his feet. "Two blasts. That's all the energy the death-hawk can fire without retreating and recharging. You okay?"

Tinker stared at his companion. Even in the moonlight, he could see that the giant's skin was covered with bright turquoise-colored scales, and his teeth flashed with a greenish glow.

"I'm not sure," Tinker said. He looked around. The moonlit brush-covered hills looked vaguely famil-iar. So did the beach in the distance. But where was he? What was he doing here? "I mean," he went on, "I don't seem to be injured."

"That's the main thing," the giant said, handing over Tinker's pack. He scanned the starry sky. "No sign of the deathhawk now. I'd sure like to know where that thing is."

The giant pointed a blue-scaled finger. "There."

Tinker looked in the indicated direction. At first, he could see nothing but twinkling stars. Then he noticed a faint blue light moving in the blackness. "That's what was shooting at us?"

"Yes, and since there's only one other person the deathhawk could be after right now, I'd say we've found Chameleon. Let's get over there before she gets herself killed."

Tinker found himself running again, with little clear sense of what was going on. He looked up and again spotted the blue glow.

"Chameleon!" the blue giant shouted when they were halfway up the hill. "Where are you?"

"You don't need to shout, Envoy." The voice came from a clump of bushes. The branches parted, and a black-haired girl stepped forward.

The giant looked dumbfounded. "If you're here," he said, "then why was the deathhawk up there?" He pointed at the bird's circling glow farther to the east.

"I made some bushes over there rustle as if I were moving through them," Chameleon said, looking pleased with herself. "I hoped that would attract the deathhawk's motion detectors, and it worked."

Tinker felt more confused than ever. "You moved the bushes half a mile away?" he said. "How?"

Chameleon pointed at a nearby bush. "Like this," she said, and the branches began to shake.

Tinker blinked, sure he was seeing things.

"Great," said the envoy, "but that trick won't fool the deathhawk twice. We'd better keep moving."

"All right," Chameleon said. Then she reached back, parted the bushes, and a man hobbled forward. But Tinker could see this was no ordinary man. He had one steel eye, and his arms and one leg were made of silvery metal. The other leg was encased in some sort of wooden support.

"Who's this?" the envoy asked suspiciously. He shook a fist at the man.

"My name is Peter," the man said, shrinking back. "I want to go with you."

"He helped me in the mines," Chameleon explained. She pointed at the wooden contraption around Peter's leg. "He broke his leg when we escaped, but I made a bush grow a cast for him." She started to lead Peter down the hill.

"You can't be serious about bringing him along!" the envoy exclaimed.

"Anyone who is Dedstorm's enemy is our friend," Chameleon said.

"But he'll slow us down!" the envoy objected.

"You sound like Dedstorm," Chameleon called back to him. "He helped me, and I won't abandon him."

"No, of course not," the envoy said. "But the fate of the galaxy is at stake! Isn't there something else—" Then his expression became anxious. "You did get it, didn't you?" he asked, starting after her. Tinker followed behind, trying to figure out what was going on.

"Of course I got it." Chameleon stopped to reach into her tunic and pull out a fist-size cube. It glowed, pulsating with a rainbow of shifting colors. "It was deep in the earth, where the Ancients had buried it long ago for safekeeping."

"What *is* that?" Tinker asked.

Chameleon gave him a funny look.

"It's the second memory cube, of course," the envoy said. Then he told Chameleon, "Tinker took a blow to the head. He doesn't seem to have his wits about him." He frowned. "Or maybe Dedstorm put some sort of spell on him."

"Dedstorm's powers depend on alien technology," Chameleon said, "not magic. He can't cast any spells. I'm the only wizard here."

Dedstorm, thought Tinker. Now that was a familiar name, a name he disliked without knowing why.

To Tinker, Chameleon said, "You do at least remember your plan, I hope?"

"Plan?"

"For rescuing Princess Nirvana from the energy wraiths."

Nirvana. Again, here was a name that was vaguely familiar. Tinker pictured a girl with chestnut hair and brown eyes. But where did he know her from? And what was an energy wraith? Tinker clenched his jaw with determination. Well, it was clear at least that these people were his friends and were depending on him.

Tinker looked from Chameleon to the envoy and back again. "We'll save her."

The envoy looked hard at Tinker, then shook his head. "You don't remember, do you? We've been under continual attack from the deathhawk. Princess Nirvana has been captured. We've gained one memory cube but lost the one Nirvana had, and now our leader has amnesia." He scanned the sky. "Keep an eye out for that mechanical deathbird, Tinker, while you try to remember who you are."

"We have a mission, the four of us—five now, counting Peter—to save the galaxy," Chameleon told him. "We're on our way to the City of the Ancients. There's a huge abandoned army of automated war machines there, the arsenal of the Ancients." Chameleon looked at him closely. "Does any of this sound familiar?"

"Vaguely," Tinker admitted.

"I am Chameleon—the wizard Chameleon. I can do things with plants, make them grow so fast that you can see them move. I can shape their vital energies and weave power webs from their life force. And this is the envoy from Deneb. We have to destroy the arsenal of the Ancients before Dedstorm can gain control of it."

"Destroy it how?" Tinker asked.

"With the memory cubes," Chameleon explained. "There are two of them. Dedstorm needs both of them to revive the arsenal and enslave humanity, but either cube can be used to destroy the arsenal and defeat him."

The envoy shook his head. "We're in for a tough time if our leader can't remember any of this."

"Dedstorm already has one of the memory cubes," Chameleon patiently continued. "Princess Nirvana was carrying it when he captured her three days ago. The princess is being held prisoner on the beach, guarded by wraiths. Sound familiar?"

Tinker nodded. The part about Dedstorm and why he needed to be stopped was clear. He resolved to get his memory back somehow. Meanwhile he could at least sound like a leader. "Fill me in on Nirvana's situation, and I'll come up with something."

The envoy said, "That sounds like the Tinker I know."

I hope so, Tinker thought to himself. The gravity of the situation was just beginning to sink in. His friends were risking their lives, depending on his leadership. Tinker straightened his pack. He wouldn't let them down.

"Deathhawk," the envoy warned, pointing.

Tinker looked up. A blue glow circled in the sky.

"With a plan or without one," Chameleon said, "let's head for the beach. If I have to be a target, I'd rather be a moving one."

Five minutes later Tinker peered through the brush that provided cover for him, Chameleon, the envoy, and the escaping cyborg named Peter. High above the hills in the east, the deathhawk circled. Tinker wondered if it had lost track of him and the others. By the light of a beach fire, Tinker could see a blanket-wrapped figure huddling close to the flames.

"Princess Nirvana," Chameleon told him.

Four shimmery figures stood on the sand behind Nirvana. They were shaped like humans, but they glowed with a faint yellow light.

"Energy wraiths," Chameleon said.

"Why would they build a fire?" the envoy asked. "Wraiths don't need to keep warm. They're projections of pure energy."

"And Dedstorm projects them from his castle, doesn't he?" Tinker said. He grinned. He had remembered something! Then he said, "No, the wraiths don't need to keep warm, but the princess does."

"True," Chameleon said. "But when has Dedstorm ever been concerned for the comfort of a captive?"

Tinker thought for a moment, then said, "The fire isn't just a source of heat. It's a source of light, too. Maybe Dedstorm wants to make sure that we see Nirvana."

Chameleon immediately understood. "A trap?"

Nodding, Tinker said, "You said a bunch of wraiths were guarding the princess. Where are all the others? Dedstorm must know we're here."

Suddenly a voice boomed through the air around them. "Brilliant deduction, Tinker," it said.

The sky lit up, and Chameleon gasped. Tinker followed her gaze upward. Projected into the night sky was Dedstorm's leering face. It was the biggest hologram Tinker had ever seen.

Holograms, he thought with a start. I have an enemy who uses holograms. But that enemy's name isn't Dedstorm, is it?

"How did he know what we were saying?" Tinker demanded.

The envoy pointed at the deathhawk. "Eyes and ears in the sky."

Peter threw himself to the ground, cowering in terror.

"It's a pity you were too cautious to walk right

into my ambush," Dedstorm said. "It would have been so convenient."

The next sound they heard came from the undergrowth—a low hum like electrical equipment about to overload. It grew louder. Something was approaching.

"Wraiths," Peter groaned miserably.

"Can't be," Chameleon said. "We'd see their glow."

"Tinker," said the envoy, "your puzzle gun!"

"My what?" Tinker asked.

"Oh, no," Chameleon moaned. "You don't remember what your puzzle gun is for?"

"It's part of your gear, Tinker," the envoy said. "In your pack. Your tools and your puzzle gun are the objects that make Tinker a tinkerer."

The buzz in the undergrowth was coming closer. And now it was clear that the sound came from both ahead and behind.

"Chip!" the envoy exclaimed. "You can ask Chip what your things are for!"

"Chip?" Tinker said, still puzzled.

"Your advisor," the envoy explained. "I've never seen him, but you talk to him. You look up, and you ask him things."

A yellow glow flashed in the underbrush off to one side. The buzz grew louder still. Another yellow light shone through the branches right in front of Tinker.

The hologram still lit up the sky. Dedstorm's huge mouth opened, showing his teeth. He laughed, and the hideous sound echoed from the nearby hills. "Time to die," he said.

Three more rectangular yellow lights emerged from the brush, and for the first time, Tinker could see clearly what they were.

Three black-clad energy wraiths stood before the three adventurers and the groveling Peter, and two more of the creatures appeared from behind. With their boots, gloves, and black scarves, the wraiths were dressed like ninja warriors. Only the area around their eyes showed through the black disguises, casting an eerie yellow haze before them.

Dedstorm said, "Only I could figure out how to use force fields to clothe energy wraiths—a mark of genius."

Like a noose tightening around the neck of a condemned man, the wraiths moved in closer and closer to Tinker and his friends. The wraiths' gloves dropped from their hands.

Tinker reached into his bag and pulled out a spool of copper wire. What good will this be? he wondered. He dropped it back inside and pulled out what looked like a bizarre battery. It was a cylinder with a notch at one end and a crease in the other. On the sides were green arrows, all pointing in one direction, and the word *Repel*. The object pulsed with milky light.

"Puzzle gun!" Tinker said in recognition. "But how—"

"Five wraiths!" the envoy cried. "Come on, Tinker. We're going to need your help!"

Tinker forced down his panic and pulled out another cylinder. This one said Focus. Desperate, he rummaged through the bag until he found the puzzle gun itself. It was shaped like some strange, brilliantly polished machine gun.

He looked up and saw the wraiths crouching, ready to spring.

Now the panic was back. With shaking hands Tinker turned the puzzle gun over. It looks familiar, his mind screamed, but how do I make it work? He took a deep breath and fit a single cylinder into the gun's slot.

At that moment a shriek ripped from the envoy's throat: "T-i-i-i-n-ker-r-r!"

Before Tinker could act, the wraiths came hurtling through the air.

7

"**H**ELP!" PETER CRIED. HE FLUNG HIMSELF AT TINker's knees, knocking him off his feet. The puzzle gun and cylinders scattered across the sandy ground.

Two wraiths grabbed for Chameleon. She dodged their outstretched arms and leapt for cover in the bushes.

The other three wraiths launched themselves at Tinker and Peter. The envoy jumped forward to intercept them and plucked two out of the air by their necks. The wraiths grappled with him, bright streams of energy coursing from their glowing hands and over the envoy's blue scales. He roared in pain.

The third wraith ducked past the envoy and faced Tinker and the cowering Peter. From behind

64

the mask of black scarves, it hissed like a deadly rattlesnake.

Tinker grabbed the puzzle gun from the sand and looked around for the cylinders. While he was distracted, the wraith charged.

"Don't let it touch you!" Peter yelled.

Too late, Tinker brandished the puzzle gun like a shield, but the wraith's fingers passed through it and gripped Tinker's left shoulder. The pain was like a hundred wasp stings, and his arm and hand went numb.

"Tinker!" Chameleon cried.

Tinker grunted with pain, then a silver hand grasped his arm and pulled him sharply backward. He landed on the sand next to Peter.

"Must be a low-energy wraith," Peter said.

"How can you tell?" Tinker asked, trying to shake some life back into his left hand.

"With a high-energy one, you'd be dead."

The wraith glowed a little less brightly now. It circled them warily.

"See?" Peter said. "You've drained it. But it's still got enough energy to kill if it grabs and holds on."

"Come on, Tinker!" the envoy shouted. "You've got to protect Peter! He can't defend himself!"

"The puzzle gun!" Chameleon cried. The bushes around her were glowing green, and the wraiths attacking her weren't able to get past the force field of vital energy. "Use the puzzle gun! Roll your eyes up! Ask Chip!"

Still shaking his hand, Tinker tried it. He looked up, and two things happened.

First, the battle scene before him seemed to shift to slow motion. Tinker could see Chameleon shaping the life energy of the bushes into a cage that trapped the wraiths attacking her. He could see the wraiths in the envoy's arms growing dimmer and dimmer as their energy drained off, coursing over the alien's blue body. He could see the fifth wraith hovering, sizing him up.

Second, a row of glowing green letters and symbols appeared in front of Tinker. Most of the symbols were meaningless to him, but the words said "Heads-up Display. To access the help chip, please say, 'Chip.' "

"Chip," Tinker said.

"Go ahead," read the letters.

"How do I use this thing?" Tinker said, gripping the puzzle gun.

After a brief pause, the green letters read, "Tinker's puzzle gun. Official name is the Logical Energy Processor. The puzzle gun processes energy by using an alien technology. As the official name implies, it operates according to logical principles."

Great, Tinker thought. I ask for advice, and I get an encyclopedia entry! The wraith above him was descending, but in slow motion.

"The device consists of the frame and trigger assembly, along with seven cylinders that alter the energy flowing from the power supply to the exit nozzle."

Yes, Tinker thought. I've got to have the cylinders.

One was just outside his reach. He stretched his hand toward it. As he looked down, away from the heads-up display, everything returned to normal motion. The wraith fell toward him.

Tinker grabbed the cylinder and kept rolling. The wraith missed him. He grabbed a second cylinder and looked up again to access Chip. Again, the action around him slowed. The two wraiths attacking the envoy were struggling fiercely to escape, clawing at his eyes. Chameleon still held her two wraiths captive, though it seemed she couldn't leave her shelter of branches, either.

"To operate the puzzle gun, place one to three cylinders in the rack, close, and lock. Then aim and pull the trigger."

A glowing diagram materialized, showing energy flowing through three puzzle gun cylinders, changing as it moved along the direction of the green arrows. "Other questions?"

The wraith had recovered and turned toward Peter.

"Not now," Tinker said, and he looked down. Suddenly everything returned to normal speed.

Peter scrambled crabwise from the wraith.

"Hang on, Peter!" Tinker said. Then, thinking aloud, he said, "The cylinders process energy in sequence." He looked at the cylinders in his hand. They were Amplify and Focus. At his feet was Repel. He scooped it up. "These should do the trick."

TOM SWIFT

He snapped the cylinders into the frame. One of them wouldn't stay put. He realized that the green arrow wasn't pointing in the right direction, so he reversed it.

Tinker heard Peter cry out in pain and saw that the wraith had grabbed his injured leg.

"No!" Tinker pulled the trigger. The nozzle of the puzzle gun shot out a bolt of white energy. It struck the wraith with the force of an electric sledgehammer. The wraith shrieked as it fell over.

Tinker shouted, too. The force of the impact jolted him backward, and he sat down hard on the ground.

"I should have seen that coming," he said. "If the puzzle gun repels something, then the gun itself is also repelled." He stood up, thinking that this might not be the best arrangement of the cylinders for a weapon.

The wraith got to its feet and turned toward Tinker. It opened its arms and the black clothes fell away. The entire glowing surface of the creature was exposed now, and he realized that every inch of it emitted deadly energy.

Frantically he scanned the ground for other cylinders.

"Uh-oh," the envoy said. "More company." Four streaks of yellow light flashed across the sky. "Reinforcement wraiths."

Tinker had no time to think about the new arrivals. The wraith he had knocked down sprinted toward him, arms open for a murderous embrace just as Peter shouted, "Catch!"

68

Tom grabbed the thrown cylinder from the air.
It was Radiate. Tinker popped out the Repel cylinder, then jammed in the new one. The new combination would make the puzzle gun a formidable
energy weapon, Tinker hoped.

He raised the weapon as the wraith made its
final leap.

He fired.

Zap! In a blaze of light, the energy wraith vanished, but the four other wraiths had flashed to
the ground. They glowed yellow, lighting up the
scene with deadly brilliance.

The wraiths that the envoy was holding
stopped struggling, then winked into nonexistence. The alien had finally drained them of their
deadly energy. He looked tired but otherwise unharmed. He gave Tinker a weary grin.

"They're like the electric jellyfish of my home
world," the envoy said. "They sting, but I can deal
with it." He grabbed two of the new arrivals and
yelled with surprise. The energy that flashed over
his scales was white-hot—even at a distance, Tinker could feel it. These must be high-energy
wraiths, he figured.

"Where's Chameleon?" Peter shouted, looking
toward the bushes where the wizard had been
holding two wraiths at bay.

Tinker looked, too. The wraiths had dissipated.
All that remained of them were their smoking
footprints. But Chameleon was gone.

"Chameleon!" Tinker shouted in dismay.

He felt searing heat near his back. He wheeled

and fired the puzzle gun once, twice. The wraiths vanished in flashes of light.

"Let me zap those two," Tinker said, aiming at the wraiths struggling in the envoy's arms.

"No!" the envoy said. "That's just what Dedstorm wants you to do. We're trying to conserve the energy in your puzzle gun, remember?"

Tinker *did* remember. The batteries in his puzzle gun contained only a certain amount of power. They drained even when the device was not in use, but using it accelerated the loss.

That wasn't all that he remembered. Dedstorm had a mostly renewable energy supply. Tinker realized that it was vital for him not to squander his own limited resources.

"You can leave these two to me." The envoy grunted, holding them by their sparking throats.

Tinker nodded and turned toward the site of Chameleon's struggle. "I'd better find Chameleon. She's carrying the second memory cube."

He glanced back at the envoy, who waved a struggling wraith in response. "Don't worry about me. I eat energy wraiths for breakfast." He licked his blue lips. "And speaking of breakfast, all this night fighting gives me a real appetite."

Leading into the underbrush, away from the bushes where Chameleon had made her stand, were the smoking footprints of wraiths, plus footprints of a more ordinary sort.

"Cyborgs," Peter said. He raised his metal foot, showing a sole that matched the marks on the ground. "They must have surprised her while she was busy with the wraiths."

"While we were *all* busy with wraiths," Tinker said. The footprints led into the scrub. "Come on. We can follow the trail of broken branches. They can't be far."

They hadn't gone more than a hundred yards when Tinker saw something on the ground that glowed with multicolored light.

"The memory cube!" Peter said. "Why would she drop that?"

Tinker picked it up. "To keep Dedstorm from getting it." From not far ahead came the sound of the cyborg abductors making their way toward the beach. "Come on!"

Once or twice Tinker thought he heard Chameleon let out a muffled cry. Soon he could see the yellow glow of wraith light.

Hang on, Chameleon, Tinker thought. I'm almost there.

When he came to a clearing, Tinker almost stepped right into the open. Just in time, he halted and pulled Peter back into the brush.

In the center of the clearing, two brightly glowing wraiths stood by while two cyborgs held Chameleon's arms. A third cyborg untied the black scarf they had used as a gag for the wizard. As the gag came free, one of the wraiths shimmered briefly and took on the form of Dedstorm himself.

A holographic projection, Tinker realized. If he hadn't seen the transformation just then, he would have mistaken the hologram for the real Dedstorm.

"All right," the image of Dedstorm said to Chameleon. "I want that memory cube, and I want it now!"

"I don't have it." Although she was in danger, Chameleon kept her voice level.

"Search her!" Dedstorm ordered the cyborgs. "And don't worry. With her hands restrained, she can't cast any spells."

Nervously the cyborgs did as they were told but found nothing.

Peter urgently whispered, "Do something, Tinker!"

Tinker raised the puzzle gun and squeezed the trigger. Nothing happened. "Something's wrong."

Dedstorm's hologram snarled. "I may look human enough," he told Chameleon, "but there's a wraith under this hologram. One touch, and you die a painful death!" His hand was poised near Chameleon's face.

"No!" Peter cried, dashing into the open.

"Halt!" the Dedstorm wraith shouted. At the sound of his former master's voice, Peter stopped.

Tinker frantically opened the puzzle gun and checked the cylinders. One was out of alignment.

"Who are you?" Dedstorm's image demanded. Then he shook his head. "No, no need to volunteer your identity. I can read your transponder. You're cyborg 7939-8. You call yourself Peter, and you are AWOL from the mines."

"Don't hurt my friend," Peter pleaded.

Dedstorm clucked as though he were scolding a child. "I don't like traitors, Peter." He looked at Chameleon and shook his head. "Taking pity on a crippled cyborg. Typical. That's why you and your friends can't defeat me. Concern for the weak is itself a weakness."

Tinker struggled to get the cylinder realigned. There was sand in the chamber. He shook it out.

The Dedstorm wraith glared at Peter. "Pathetic."

"Leave him alone!" Chameleon shouted. "Haven't you done enough?"

"No," Dedstorm said, smiling. "Not quite. Say goodbye, Peter."

With a strangled gasp, Peter clutched his chest and fell to his knees.

Tinker shouted Peter's name, snapped the puzzle gun's rack shut, and dashed to Peter's side.

"Welcome, Tinker," Dedstorm said. "Behold the future of the human race. When I rule the galaxy, all men and women will be cyborgs, and they will not dare to disobey me as this one has."

"Help me, Tinker!" Peter begged. Kneeling beside him, Tinker steadied his new friend.

"Too late, Tinker. Too late. Peter carries an implant next to his heart," Dedstorm said. "It's an array of wires that I control remotely. And by turning a dial on my belt"—he twisted the dial—"I send a jolt straight into him."

Peter cried out, his face contorted with pain. He clawed at his chest.

"Now the defective weakling will no longer annoy me."

Tinker was helpless to do anything but catch Peter as the man-machine collapsed into his arms.

Tinker lowered Peter's lifeless form but couldn't take his eyes from the body. His heart was in his throat.

"Stay right where you are, Tinker." The deadly fingers hovered near Chameleon's face again. She struggled to turn away, but the cyborgs held her fast. "Your turn now, wizard girl. Tell me where the cube is, or die!"

8

I HAVE THE CUBE," TINKER SAID QUIETLY AS HE straightened up. He put his hand inside his vest and touched the cube.

"Then save your friend," said Dedstorm's hologram. "Hand it over."

Tinker brought out the cube and stepped closer to the disguised wraith.

"Tinker, don't!" Chameleon cried.

With one hand Tinker extended the cube so that the wraith had to reach for it with the same hand that threatened Chameleon. Then, with his other hand, Tinker leveled the puzzle gun and fingered the trigger. He held his breath and hoped that the cylinders were properly aligned.

Tinker fired. In a brilliant flash, the Dedstorm wraith disappeared.

75

Chameleon struggled free from the surprised cyborgs and sprinted clear.

The second wraith flickered and took on Dedstorm's form. "Attack him!" he commanded the cyborgs.

Tinker pulled the trigger again, and the second Dedstorm wraith also vanished. For a moment, Tinker thought that the three cyborgs might try to rush him. Then Chameleon waved her hands, and the grass beneath their feet grew so quickly and tangled so tightly around their ankles that they could hardly move. When they were able to pull their feet free, they bolted to the far end of the clearing.

"That was quite unmannerly of you, Tinker." Dedstorm's voice boomed through the night air as the huge image of his face formed again in the night sky. "I suppose you think you've managed some sort of victory here." The enormous face smiled hideously. "But what about your blue-skinned friend? He's a terror against wraiths, but he can't do much against four cyborgs who know how to obey orders."

The stars filled the sky again.

"Oh, no!" Chameleon whispered.

In the silence, Chameleon shaped some bushes into a bier for Peter, his final resting place. Then they slowly made their way back. Tinker saw no sign of the envoy, other than broken branches—evidence of a hard-fought struggle. The blue-skinned giant's pack lay on the ground, and some of his food supplies had spilled out. Tinker picked up the food and the rest of the fallen cylinders.

Chameleon said, "They can't have taken him far."

Tinker shook his head. "Actually," he said, "they could have covered a lot of territory by now, assuming that they attacked the envoy soon after I left." He handed his own pack to Chameleon and hefted the envoy's onto his back. He stifled a moan when the pack's heavy strap cut into his wraith-burned shoulder.

"Can we track them?"

"Possibly," Tinker said. "But what about the princess?" He looked back at the beach, where the fire was still burning.

"Well," Chameleon said, "why don't I look for the envoy while you rescue the princess? The wraiths guarding Nirvana can't be very strong now."

"No, we can't split up. That's what Dedstorm wants. We can't let him divide us the way he did last time."

"Last time?" Chameleon said. "What last time?"

Tinker frowned and scratched his head. What had he meant by that? Had he and his friends faced Dedstorm before? No, of course not.

Tinker shrugged. "I don't know why I said that," he said, "but I do know that we can't separate. The princess is probably half starved. We've got to rescue her first."

"Okay," Chameleon said unhappily. "But I hate leaving the envoy behind."

"So do I," Tinker said.

They advanced cautiously toward the firelit beach, but when Tinker peered through the underbrush, he saw that they were too late. The fire still burned, but Nirvana and the wraiths were gone. Footprints led into the dunes, and they followed these until the ground grew too hard to show any trace.

"Now what?" Chameleon asked.

Tinker looked in vain for the yellow wraith glow.

"Well," he said, "let's see what I've got here." He took his tinker's bag from Chameleon and dumped its contents onto the ground. Moonlight gleamed on the spool of wire, the rope, the nuts and bolts, the pliers and wire cutters and screwdrivers and puzzle gun cylinders that made up his supplies.

"Here," he said, picking a cylinder. "This one looks promising." The cylinder said Sympathize.

Chameleon squinted at it. "The puzzle gun is going to feel sorry for us?"

Tinker grinned and loaded the cylinder. "Well, that's one meaning of the word. But I'm betting that in this case, it has more to do with physics than with emotion. When one object vibrates, it can cause another object to move in the same manner. That's called sympathetic vibration."

Next, Tinker inserted the Focus and Amplify cylinders into the frame. He cut a length of wire and looped it around the back of the Amplify cylinder so that it would vibrate with that cylinder's energy. Then he pulled the trigger of the puzzle gun and swept the nozzle from left to right.

At first nothing seemed to be happening, but then the Amplify cylinder and wire vibrated with sound. It was the low, electric hum of wraith energy. Tinker had created a device that captured and reproduced distant sounds. He moved the puzzle gun from side to side until he found the direction of the loudest hum.

"This way," Tinker said, pointing toward the hills.

He quickly tossed his tools in his bag and handed it to Chameleon. Then he hefted the envoy's pack onto his own shoulder, and they were off.

As they crested the second hill, Tinker stopped. Below him were the fleeing wraiths, but their progress was slow. Tinker saw Princess Nirvana stumbling along in front of them, obviously weary. The wraiths weren't any more energetic. All four flickered as if they would soon wink out.

Chameleon pointed to the princess. "Look, Tinker, Nirvana's still wearing her bracers."

Seeing Tinker's puzzled look, she explained. "The bracers are bands of exotic metal alloys and electronics covering her wrists and forearms. If her hands weren't tied behind her back, she could use her bracers to destroy the wraiths."

Tinker nodded.

"Can we free her without using any more of your puzzle gun energy?" Chameleon whispered.

"I think so," Tinker said. "Here." He dug a small knife from his tinker's bag and quickly outlined a plan to Chameleon.

* * *

The princess and the wraiths all turned at once when Tinker stepped out into the open a short distance behind them.

"That's far enough," Tinker said, leveling his puzzle gun.

"Tinker!" Dark rings of exhaustion showed under Nirvana's brown eyes, but her weariness seemed to fall away as she smiled.

"Hi, Nirvana," he said. "I'm your rescue party. These wraiths are history." He pulled the puzzle gun trigger.

Nothing happened.

"Oops." Tinker grinned nervously and started to back away. "Say, wraiths wouldn't attack an unarmed man, would they?"

All four wraiths hissed in unison and began advancing toward Tinker.

"Tinker!" Nirvana said again, her smile fading.

"Not to worry!" Chameleon said as she snatched Nirvana from behind the distracted wraiths. She pulled the princess into the protection of branches that started to glow with magical force.

Realizing that they had been tricked, the wraiths turned and hissed again. They surrounded the bush, but Chameleon's shield of green energy held firmly against them.

Then, suddenly, the bush lost its green glow. One wraith, emitting a crackle that passed for laughter, reached into the bush.

Nirvana, with pieces of severed rope still clinging to her wrists, stood up and slammed her bracers down on the wraith's head. With a shower of sparks, the wraith winked out.

Tinker, meanwhile, had repaired his intentional sabotage of the puzzle gun. He zapped another wraith as it reached for Nirvana.

"Thanks, Tinker," the princess said as she stepped into the open. Now just two wraiths were left.

The energy creatures hesitated for a moment, as though deciding what to do. Then both leapt toward the bush where Chameleon was still hidden, hoping, it seemed, to surprise her.

It didn't work. Chameleon restored her shield of vital energy, and Nirvana struck one wraith from behind with her bracers. The first blow stunned it. It turned toward her, hissing.

Tinker shot the second wraith, dissipating it. The first recovered and opened its arms to embrace Nirvana. But Nirvana stood between Tinker and the wraith—he couldn't fire to save her.

With a triumphant yell, Nirvana swung her forearms beneath the wraith's closing arms and struck its midsection. This time there were no sparks. The wraith disappeared like a candle flame in a sudden wind.

Nirvana's first act of freedom was to wrap her arms around Tinker in a grateful hug. Tinker felt his face get hot with embarrassment.

The princess released him. "This is going to make me sound a lot like the envoy," she said, "but are you guys as hungry as I am?"

"Yes," Tinker said, dragging the envoy's well-supplied pack from the undergrowth. "And there's nothing I'd like better than to lighten this load!"

While they ate, Chameleon asked, "How's the puzzle gun holding out?"

"I'll see," Tinker said. He rolled his gaze upward and softly said, "Chip." Glowing green letters formed and responded to his question—the puzzle gun was down to thirty-eight percent of its full charge.

"Not good," he reported. Then, seeing the dismay on Chameleon's face, he added, "but not so terrible, either. We'll be okay."

Overhead, the night sky flickered with light. Dedstorm's features appeared against the stars. "Ah," said the villainous face, "the mark of a true leader. Putting the best light on a hopeless situation."

Chameleon jumped with surprise, and Nirvana dropped the dried fruit she had been about to eat.

Dedstorm sneered. His voice this time was barely above a whisper, which made it seem that he was right there with them. "Not that it will do you any good."

How had Dedstorm known what they were—

Tinker knew the answer before he finished the thought. The deathhawk. Tinker scanned the sky warily. If that mysterious bird was close enough to hear his every word, then it was close enough to attack with deadly accuracy.

Calmly, as if he were merely fiddling with the puzzle gun out of curiosity, Tinker began to reconfigure the device. He removed the copper wire, and he put the Focus and Sympathize cylinders back into his bag.

"I have Nirvana's memory cube," Dedstorm reminded Tinker and the others, "and I want Chameleon's, too. But I can't expect you to be reasonable and just hand over what I want, can I?"

Tinker found the cylinders labeled Repel and Disperse, but then Repel slipped from his fingers and dropped back into the bag. Fishing for it, Tinker scanned the illuminated sky again for the blue glow of the deathhawk.

"I have something else that might interest you," Dedstorm said. "The envoy. And I have plans for him—unpleasant plans." The face in the sky grimaced wickedly.

"Where are you holding him?" Tinker demanded. His fingers closed around a cylinder. Was it the right one?

"Meet me in the Canyon of the Ancients," Dedstorm answered. "Then perhaps you can save your friend. Assuming, that is, that nothing unfortunate happens to you along the way."

The image of Dedstorm faded from the sky. Tinker noticed a smudge of gray light in the east. Dawn was coming.

Then Tinker noticed something else: a flash of blue light low in the sky.

"Deathhawk!" Tinker warned.

9

CHAMELEON AND NIRVANA DIVED FOR COVER just as a brilliant bolt of deadly energy shot down directly at Tinker.

Meanwhile Tinker jammed the cylinder in his hand into the puzzle gun. He raised the device and pulled the trigger just as the ground exploded at his feet.

An umbrella-shaped shield shot out toward the deathhawk. The evil bird struck the shield like a sparrow flying into a window. But the shield didn't block its energy bolts completely. The shock of the explosion at his feet threw Tinker backward into a bush, and for a moment he was dazed. He shook his head clear and scanned the skies. No sign of the deathhawk.

"All right!" Nirvana cheered. "Great job, Tinker!" She stepped out from the bush where she had taken cover.

"Thanks," Tinker said, getting to his feet. He didn't bother to mention how lucky he'd been. If he hadn't slotted the right cylinder into the puzzle gun, that bolt would have killed him.

"I think the deathhawk went down," Chameleon said, brushing the dirt from her shoulders. "Maybe you took care of that thing for good, Tinker."

But a moment later, they all saw a blue glow rise unsteadily into the sky. It was the deathhawk flying erratically away.

Tinker looked at Chameleon with a fading smile and shrugged.

"So," Chameleon said. "Are we going to the Canyon of the Ancients as Dedstorm expects us to?"

"What choice do we have?" Tinker said. "If there's a chance of rescuing the envoy, we have to take it."

The trio headed east, toward the rising sun and the Canyon of the Ancients. Tinker asked Chip for a map of the region. Traveling through the canyon would bring them closer to Dedstorm's castle, closer to the source of his power. The route would also bring them closer to the City of the Ancients, where the arsenal of the Ancients was hidden underground.

Nirvana glanced at Tinker as they walked. "This is a trap," Nirvana said with conviction, "another opportunity for Dedstorm to drain some more of your puzzle gun's energy."

"Right," Tinker agreed. "But this time we're going to turn the situation to our advantage."

"How?" Nirvana and Chameleon said at once.

"I don't know," Tinker admitted. "We'll figure it out when we see what we're faced with."

Despite his confident words, Tinker was worried. Dedstorm had a surprising amount of energy. To project his holograms, to send his energy wraiths into battle, to power his deathhawk, Dedstorm had already used more energy than Tinker's puzzle gun had contained at its fullest charge.

Dedstorm had a tremendous energy advantage. With a sinking feeling, Tinker couldn't forget that if he couldn't find a way to stop Dedstorm before his own energy ran out, the villain would put an end to human freedom in the galaxy.

An hour after dawn, with the hills growing steeper around them, Tinker decided the group should stop to rest. Chameleon volunteered to take the first watch while the others dozed. For Tinker, it had been a long night. As soon as he settled down in a grassy patch, he fell asleep.

It seemed that he had closed his eyes for only a moment when Chameleon was shaking his shoulder, telling him it was his turn to watch. He did feel rested, though, and the sun had certainly climbed higher in the sky.

"I almost feel as if I didn't sleep," Tinker said, standing up and stretching. "And I didn't dream."

"Of course you dreamed," Chameleon said, settling down on Tinker's spot. "You just don't remember what you dreamed."

"Maybe you're right," Tinker said. He stretched again.

"Mmm-hmm," Chameleon mumbled, already half asleep.

Tinker bent to gather up his things, and in an instant, he did remember something—a dream of the distant past, a dream of Old Earth in the time before the Ancients. In the dream Tinker was sitting on a beach with Chameleon and Nirvana, only the two girls were somehow different.

Another dream image surfaced. Tinker remembered seeing a pile of small but powerful batteries in a smoky room. Blue sparks jumped and glittered across the surface of these batteries. It was a display of pre-Ancient technology, the form of energy called electricity, which Dedstorm also commanded.

Tinker looked at his puzzle gun and realized that, for some reason, he seemed to remember a lot about electricity. That was odd. The alien technology of the puzzle gun was still a total mystery to him.

Tinker shook his head to clear it of strange dreams. This was no time to think about things that weren't real.

Tinker looked around at the trio's encampment. This was real. The encampment was on a little rise of ground, and Tinker began to walk in a circle, looking up at the steepening slopes on either side. It was clear that they were near the mouth of the canyon. He saw no sign of the deathhawk in the cloudless sky. Perhaps even Dedstorm was resting.

Dedstorm, too, was real, Tinker thought to himself. How could he defeat Dedstorm? How much energy did he still have to work with?

"Chip," he said aloud, rolling his gaze upward. "What's the current status of the puzzle gun?"

Immediately he saw the green letters as if they were floating in the air. "Your batteries are drained to thirty-five percent of full charge." There was a pause. "Resuming real-time display now." Then Chip was gone.

Tinker resumed his pacing. Nirvana and Chameleon slept on. The sun climbed higher in the sky, and Tinker's boots were beginning to wear a path in the ground when a strange sound made him stop and look around.

Ka-thump!

Chameleon and Nirvana both sat up, startled. They looked at Tinker, then at each other. Nirvana started to say, "What was—"

Kata-thump, kata-thump, kata-kata-kata-thump.

"A drum!" Chameleon said.

The drumbeat was joined by the sound of an electric bass guitar, and then another guitar picked up the melody.

"It's coming from over there," Nirvana said, pointing toward the mouth of the canyon.

"Well, what are we waiting for?" Tinker said. "Let's see what it is."

They didn't have to go far to see the source of the sound. An enormous pile of junk sat in a clearing just outside the Canyon of the Ancients. On top of the pile, among fenders and wheels and discarded gearboxes, were four moving mannequins. Three held guitars, and the fourth was playing the drums.

As Tinker and his companions drew closer, they could see that one of the figures wasn't a mannequin at all.

"Prince Satori!" Nirvana said, running toward the junk pile. "What are you doing here?"

"Playing music!" the figure with long, dark curly hair said. He nodded toward the three robot musicians. "This is my band, the Scavenged Parts."

The robot musicians all waved.

"You know this guy?" Tinker said, surprised.

"Chameleon, Tinker," said Nirvana, "meet Prince Satori, my cousin."

"And official court musician to Dedstorm, soon to be emperor of the galaxy!" Satori played a fanfarelike riff on his guitar.

"You're on Dedstorm's side?" Nirvana said, dismayed.

"Hey," Prince Satori said. "Always go with a winner. I'm writing a song for Dedstorm. It's called 'The Undefeated.' Want to hear it?"

"No!" Nirvana said. "I can't believe you'd team up with such a villain!"

"And I can't believe you'd cling to a loser like Tinker," Satori shot back. "Just look at what Dedstorm has done for my band." He patted the chrome that came up to his waist. "It's all me! Everything you see here"—he pointed at the robots—"my brain controls them. Dedstorm made me a music cyborg, a one-man band!"

The Scavenged Parts played a few chords of nerve-shattering heavy metal.

"Dedstorm is evil," Nirvana argued.

"Most of his cyborgs are slaves," Chameleon added. "They live miserable lives, and he kills them if they disobey."

"You're getting all emotional," Satori said. "I'm past all of that. The strong rule the weak. That's life. Hey, want to hear Dedstorm's victory song?"

"No!" Nirvana shouted. To the others she said, "Let's get out of here."

Tinker opened his mouth to say something, but knew he wouldn't be heard over the band. He shrugged, then he and Chameleon followed Nirvana as she strode quickly into the mouth of the canyon.

"Who is the master of the galaxy?" Satori sang. "Who rules from zero to infinity?"

The music wasn't bad, but the lyrics made Tinker and his companions press their hands over their ears. They kept walking, and soon the Scavenged Parts were only a distant rumble. The trail rose from the floor of the Canyon of the Ancients to follow a ledge along one wall. The farther they went, the higher they climbed.

Tinker suddenly stopped. "Look down there!" he said.

Below them stretched the abandoned City of the Ancients. Trees and shrubs grew right to the edge of the city's plain, but the land around the city itself was barren. The ground looked as flat and hard as concrete.

"Over there!" Nirvana said, pointing. Within sight of the city was Dedstorm's castle—a menacing monolith that bristled with battered steel-and-glass towers.

"Well," a familiar voice called out, "it took you long enough to get here!"

On the opposite side of the canyon ran a ledge like the one on which Tinker's group stood. There, arms folded, was Dedstorm leaning against a piece of machinery that appeared to be some sort of projector. He leered across the canyon at them.

"I brought your friend," the archvillain said. He pointed to the other side of the machine.

Tinker peered across the divide at the place Dedstorm was pointing to. Partially hidden by Dedstorm's device was the large blue form of the envoy, trussed like a bird for roasting. Tinker stared hard at him, straining to catch the slightest flicker of movement. But the envoy's eyes stayed closed, and his massive body remained still and stiff—and dead.

10

WHAT I PROPOSE," DEDSTORM SAID, LEANING against his strange piece of machinery, "is a game—a contest between myself and Tinker. A little one-on-one." He smiled wickedly. "A sporting chance for you, just to be fair."

"Just what do you have in mind?" Tinker said, not taking his eyes from the envoy's motionless body.

Dedstorm flicked a switch on his machine. Tinker, Chameleon, and Nirvana all leapt back as the device shot a beam of energy across the canyon.

Dedstorm gestured toward the machine, then toward the energy beam. "This is my newest invention, the projection bridge." He stepped out onto the beam. It supported his weight just as a solid footbridge would.

"You didn't invent that at all," Nirvana scoffed. "Projection bridges are alien technology, just like Tinker's puzzle gun. There's a projection bridge at the entrance to my father's castle."

"I restored this one from a broken relic. Let's say I reinvented it. Or let's say—"

"Just tell us about this contest," Tinker broke in.

"Of course," Dedstorm said. "It's very simple, Tinker. We'll both step out onto the bridge. Just the two of us. For my only weapon, I'll have my power belt." He hooked his thumbs inside the belt. "You'll have your puzzle gun. We'll be evenly matched. You try to cross to my side. If you succeed, then I'll release your blue friend here. If you fail . . ." He looked at the envoy and shook his head. "But perhaps you don't think he's worth saving."

Tinker gritted his teeth. "He's worth it," he said, "but how do I know he's even alive?"

"Oh, he's alive, all right." Dedstorm stepped around the energy bridge's projector and nudged the envoy with his foot. "But you see, the envoy's species requires food almost constantly. Starve them for a while, and they go comatose." He took a tiny bottle from inside his belt, unstoppered it, and showed Tinker the glass dropper.

"Sugar water," Dedstorm said, leaning over the envoy. He opened the alien's jaw and let a drop fall onto the blue tongue.

To Tinker's relief, the envoy stirred.

"A few more drops," Dedstorm said, squeezing the bulb of the dropper, "and he almost revives."

The envoy opened his eyes and tried to sit up. He looked disoriented.

"Without more food," Dedstorm said, "he'll soon pass out again. And if he goes much longer without nourishment, nothing will revive him."

"All right," Tinker said, his voice hard. "I accept your challenge."

"Excellent."

"No, Tinker!" Nirvana cried.

Tinker looked at the envoy, whose eyes were already closing again. "What choice do I have? I can't let the envoy starve!"

"I remind you," Dedstorm said, "that this is to be a contest of honor, between just us two."

"Honor," Nirvana said under her breath. "He's one to talk about honor. There's hardly a government on this planet that Dedstorm hasn't betrayed or corrupted in some way, Tinker. You can't trust him!"

"I know that," Tinker whispered back, "and I know that this is just a trick to get me to drain my puzzle gun. But I don't see any other way to help the envoy." He rummaged through his bag. "I'd better not take all of this stuff with me. Just the gun and the cylinders."

He put four cylinders in the front pockets of his leather tinker's vest. Then he took the other three and configured the puzzle gun to Amplify, Shape, and Disperse. Tinker strapped the device to his forearm, then ran a length of wire from his belt to the trigger. He could start the energy flowing by thrusting his arm forward, and his hands would remain free. "I hope this works."

"Listen, Tinker," Chameleon said, "as soon as Dedstorm thinks you're winning, he'll cheat."

"I know," Tinker said, looking overhead for the deathhawk. "He may be cheating already. Who knows if that's really Dedstorm? But we may still have an advantage. Tell me, has either of you noticed anything strange about the deathhawk?"

Chameleon and Nirvana exchanged curious glances.

"At night the deathhawk doesn't cast the yellow glow that's typical of alien technology. It glows blue, like an overflow of ordinary electricity." Tinker took out his spool of copper wire and a handful of nuts and bolts. "Which of you has the better throwing arm?" he asked.

Moments later, with the puzzle gun firmly strapped to his arm, Tinker stepped out onto the shimmering energy bridge. From the opposite side Dedstorm advanced, though only a short distance.

Tinker looked down over the edge of the bridge. Far below he could see the jagged rocks and tall trees, and his stomach knotted.

"It's a long way to fall, isn't it?" Dedstorm said. "And there aren't any railings or handholds on this bridge, Tinker. I do hope you won't slip."

Tinker looked up at his opponent. "I won't."

Dedstorm laughed. "We'll see," he said. He moved the disks on one side of his belt. Like the puzzle gun, Dedstorm's power belt could be configured to use energy many different ways.

"How about a dose of raw energy, Tinker?" Dedstorm said, raising his hands.

With a flash, a ball of light appeared between Dedstorm's palms. Tinker twisted to one side, and the wire pulled the puzzle gun trigger. Tinker felt his own hands tingle with energy.

He had barely recovered when an energy bolt shot from Dedstorm's fingertips.

Reacting with lightning speed, Tinker raised his hands palms outward and shaped a field of dispersing energy. Dedstorm's potentially deadly bolt expanded into brilliant but harmless light.

"That's an amazing little device of yours," Dedstorm said. "You always manage to find just the right combination of cylinders for it, don't you?"

Tinker took another step forward, then another. Then one more.

"Almost halfway," Dedstorm said. "But look down again, Tinker. Take a good look at how far you're going to fall."

Tinker kept his eyes on Dedstorm and took another step.

"You're not looking down, Tinker. Is it because you're afraid of heights?"

"You're not going to psych me out," Tinker said, taking one more careful step. He could feel his breaths coming fast and shallow.

Dedstorm moved the disks on his belt again. "Oh, I don't need psychology, Tinker. I'm going to do you in with physics." Dedstorm put his hands on the surface of the energy bridge. "Do you surf, Tinker? How'd you like to catch some waves?"

Dedstorm's hands began to vibrate, and the vibrations traveled into the bridge. Where Dedstorm was kneeling, the bridge was calm, but in front of him the vibrations became tiny waves, and the waves traveled toward Tinker.

Tinker felt the vibrations only in his toes at first. Then the ripples grew larger, and Tinker fell to his knees.

"Hang on, Tinker!" Chameleon shouted.

"Yes, Tinker," Dedstorm sneered. "Do hang on. Try not to think about that long, long fall to the bottom, or the hard, hard ground that awaits you." His hand motions became more violent, creating waves that were faster and stronger.

As he was jolted up and down Tinker ejected two of his puzzle gun cylinders, managed to stuff them into his vest, and replaced them with Sympathize and Repel. He wanted to leave the Shape cylinder in place, but the vibrations caused it to pop out on its own. Fighting the waves and his rising nausea, Tinker couldn't hold his hand steady enough to get the last cylinder back into place.

"Are you trying to make that thing into a parachute?" Dedstorm said, whipping the energy bridge up and down with all his strength. "You'd better hurry!"

The waves were now lifting Tinker into the air,

dropping him hard onto the bridge, and lifting him again.

"Tell Chameleon to hand over the remaining memory cube," Dedstorm shouted, "and you'll live!"

"She . . . wouldn't . . . give . . . it . . . to . . . you!" Tinker said as the waves tossed him higher each time. Finally he snapped the Shape cylinder into place. "And . . . we . . . won't . . . quit!" He closed the rack and put both hands on the bridge. He shot his arm forward. The wire between his belt and the puzzle gun trigger grew taut, and the device hummed to life.

The energy bridge vibrated under Tinker's hands. He started to shape the waves as Dedstorm had done but out of phase with Dedstorm's rhythm. The two wave forms canceled, and the bridge became steady again.

Dedstorm stood with a disgusted look on his face. He reached toward his belt and changed its configuration again.

Tinker rushed forward, grabbing puzzle gun cylinders from his vest as he ran.

Already a ball of light was forming in Dedstorm's hands.

"Go, Tinker!" Chameleon shouted. He was almost across the bridge now.

"No, you don't!" Dedstorm cried. Another energy bolt flew from his hands. Tinker activated the newly configured puzzle gun. As before, he caught the deadly energy with his hands and shaped it into harmless light.

From the corner of his eye, though, Tinker caught a flash of movement in the air above.

"Deathhawk!" Chameleon warned, just as the robotic bird swooped down and blasted out a beam of energy.

At this range, Tinker knew, the deathhawk couldn't miss. He reshaped his energy field just in time. The bolt scattered brilliant flares of light around Tinker, blinding him.

"I thought you said this would be between just the two of us," Tinker said between his teeth.

"So I lied," Dedstorm said. "And I'll win!" He reshaped the bridge so that it formed a sheer wall in front of Tinker. "Did you really think I'd fight fair?"

Tinker watched the deathhawk make a wide turn farther down the canyon. It wouldn't be hard to absorb another attack, but Tinker worried about what all of this was costing him in puzzle gun energy. Even if he could still save the envoy, Tinker knew he couldn't be much help to the others if the puzzle gun was useless.

The deathhawk started back, flying alongside the canyon wall. Tinker saw his chance. He thought, If I can just get it to fly a little closer to Chameleon and Nirvana . . .

"All right, Dedstorm," Tinker said. "If the rules are suspended for you, then they're suspended for me." He sprinted back toward his friends.

As the deathhawk turned toward Tinker and swept close to the girls, Tinker threw himself flat onto the bridge and shouted, "Now, Nirvana! Now!"

The princess threw the assembly of bolts and wire into the air in front of the deathhawk. The deadly raptor flew into the wire mesh at one end, while the weighted spool unraveled at the other, sending the bare wire down, down, down.

The deathhawk flew on, continuing to build up enough electrical charge for another attack. The air around its head began to glow.

Then the trailing wire made contact with the ground.

Like a lightning bolt, the deathhawk's electric charge shot into the ground. The sudden, uncontrolled discharge scrambled the bird's electronic brain. Its wings folded, and it plummeted to the rocks below.

"No!" Dedstorm cried. He retreated a few steps, then adjusted his power belt. "You'll pay for that, Tinker!"

Hands on his belt, Dedstorm adjusted the shape of the bridge. The part where Tinker was standing began to shrink from both sides, narrowing into nothing.

"All right," Tinker said, unstrapping the puzzle gun from his arm. He ejected all of the cylinders, dropping one in his haste. "If I fall, Dedstorm, we both fall!"

He aimed the puzzle gun nozzle at the energy bridge's projector. Squeezing the trigger, he sent a stream of pure energy into the machine.

The projector's hum turned shrill.

"No, you fool!" Dedstorm cried. "You'll over-load it!"

"Exactly!"

With that, the energy bridge winked out.

For half a heartbeat, Tinker and Dedstorm seemed to be hanging in midair.

Then they were both hurtling downward to be smashed on the jagged rocks below.

11

TINKER HAD JUST SECONDS TO RECONFIGURE the puzzle gun. He slotted the Repel cylinder, then fumbled with the Disperse cylinder. It slipped out of his fingers.

He saw the canyon floor rushing up at him, then turned his head to see the energy bridge flicker back to life as its circuits adjusted for the overload. Like a rubber band of yellow light, the bridge looped down into the canyon and caught Dedstorm.

Fortunately, Tinker and the Disperse cylinder fell at the same rate. He snatched it out of the air and slotted it into the puzzle gun.

Snapping the gun shut, Tinker aimed the nozzle down and pulled the trigger. A weak energy field spread out below. Like a sudden wind, it rippled through the trees and stirred the dust on the canyon floor. Tinker felt himself slow gradually as the field built up resistance between the puzzle gun and the ground. He had to grip the puzzle gun tightly to keep it from being ripped from his arm.

When he finally tumbled onto the canyon floor, the air was thick with dust. The dispersed energy of Tinker's fall had kicked up bits of old leaves and pine needles. Tinker coughed and brushed himself off.

"Very clever." Dedstorm's voice came from above. "Very clever indeed."

The energy bridge was functioning again. Now it hung down several hundred feet into the canyon like an extra long rope bridge. Dedstorm stood on the bottom loop like a child on an oversize swing.

"You do manage some ingenious things with that puzzle gun," Dedstorm said. "I admire you. Just a little bit." He twisted a dial on his belt, and the energy bridge began to swing back and forth. "That won't keep me from finishing you off, of course." He twisted the dial again, and the center of the bridge rippled, then thickened. With a sick feeling Tinker saw that Dedstorm was turning the bridge into a giant, swinging battering ram.

With each swing, the bridge came closer to where Tinker stood. Tinker stepped backward, into a solid rock wall.

Too late he realized that the canyon opened at only one end—the end opposite to where he was. And the cliff at his back was too steep to climb.

Dedstorm laughed with pleasure as the bridge

arced even closer to Tinker, who searched in his vest for a new set of cylinders.

"That's right, use your toy!" Dedstorm cried triumphantly, holding on tight as the bridge swung murderously toward Tinker. "It has enough energy to shield you a few times. But then . . ."

Tinker frowned. The Amplify cylinder was gone.

"Then," Dedstorm called out, swinging forward again, "I'll crush you like an ant under a hammer!"

Suddenly the energy bridge vanished. Dedstorm's momentum, however, kept carrying him forward through the air. He landed in a bush with a crash.

Tinker looked up to see Chameleon waving from above. She pointed at the energy-bridge projector. There were bushes growing up around it, and even from a distance, Tinker could see that some of the branches had grown into the machinery, expanded within it, and destroyed it.

Smiling, Tinker turned toward Dedstorm and said, "You were saying?" But where he expected Dedstorm, a robot stood.

"You and your holograms," Tinker said through his teeth. Then he noticed that the robot was wearing Dedstorm's power belt. Of course! Tinker realized with pleasure that a hologram projection of the belt wouldn't have been enough to operate the bridge. The robot had to wear the genuine article.

Tinker raised the puzzle gun. At least if he destroyed the robot now, Dedstorm would lose his precious belt.

"You've forgotten," Dedstorm said as his hologram flickered back into place. "You have the puzzle gun configured as a shock absorber, not a weapon." He bent to pick something up from the ground. Then the top half of Dedstorm's robot body detached and lifted off on twin rocket exhausts.

"Don't think I'm beaten!" Dedstorm shouted. "No plants grow around the City of the Ancients, so Chameleon's tricks won't help you. And neither will this!"

The top half of the robot streaked away with the belt. In one hand, the robot waved the missing Amplify cylinder.

Meanwhile Tinker heard a mechanical voice from the bottom half of the robot softly counting down: "Four . . . three . . . two . . ."

Expecting the worst, Tinker braced himself against the canyon wall and pulled the puzzle gun trigger. The shock-absorbing field repelled the robot's bottom half, sending it flying.

Then the bomb in the robot legs detonated with a bone-jarring explosion.

"Are you all right?" Tinker recognized Nirvana's voice. He opened his eyes and saw her and Chameleon anxiously bending over him. Looking around, he saw that he was still at the bottom of the canyon.

Tinker shook the cobwebs from his head. His

ears were still ringing, and his wraith-burned shoulder ached. "How's the envoy?" he asked.

"We'll show you," Chameleon said as she and Nirvana helped Tinker to his feet. Together they supported him as he stumbled out of the canyon and back onto the trail.

"Wonderful," the envoy told Tinker a little later. He took a sip from a wooden bowl. "Nirvana, what is this?"

"Flower nectar." Nirvana pointed to a place farther up the trail where Chameleon was now running her fingers over some plant stalks. "She's making the plants bloom in a hurry and produce an extra supply of nectar. It was the only way to feed you while you were unconscious."

Tinker knelt beside the alien. He had noticed the envoy was now wearing a glowing collar around his neck. Was this another of Dedstorm's tricks?

"This nectar really is wonderful," the envoy said, licking his lips. "But it isn't filling, exactly. What I'd really like is something that would stick to my ribs."

Nirvana laughed. "We thought you'd say something like that." She handed the envoy another bowl. This one was heaped with pine nuts.

"Excellent!" the envoy said. He poured the bowl's contents into his mouth and started to gnash the nuts between his massive teeth. "Another five or six bowls like this, and I'll be fully restored."

Just then Chameleon returned with another bowl of flower nectar.

"He wants more nuts," Tinker told her.

Chameleon put her hand on the envoy's shoulder. "I never thought I'd say this, but I'm happy to see that you have an appetite." Then to Tinker she said, "Come on. You can help me get some more pine nuts."

As soon as she and Tinker were out of earshot, Chameleon said, "What is that thing around his neck?"

Tinker shook his head. "I don't know. It seems to be made of plasteel, the same material my puzzle gun cylinders are made of."

"I'm worried." The wizard sighed. "There's something else, too." She stopped and touched a pine tree. Nut-bearing cones visibly began to grow on the branches above, but the rate of growth slowed as Tinker and Chameleon watched.

"My power is weakening," Chameleon said. She nodded at the tree. "By now nuts should be raining down on our heads, but the cones are only half-formed."

Chameleon looked over her shoulder at the side of the canyon they had come from. "Back there," she said, "when I made those bushes grow into Dedstorm's bridge projector, I was worried that the branches wouldn't grow fast enough to wreck the machine in time to save you."

She patted the tree trunk. "I think it has to do with the powers of the Ancients. The energy they used for their weapons poisoned the land with some kind of radiation. That's why the ground is so stony and barren around the abandoned city.

The closer we get to the arsenal of the Ancients, the more the ground and plants are poisoned."

"And the devices that caused this—those are the drone weapons that Dedstorm wants to reactivate?" Tinker shook his head.

"Tinker! Chameleon!" The panicked cry came from Nirvana.

They whipped around to see the envoy thrashing on the ground, his huge hands clawing at his neck. Nirvana was trying without success to help him.

"It's the neck ring," she shouted. "It's choking him!"

CHAMELEON AND TINKER RACED BACK, BUT BY the time they reached the envoy's side, he had collapsed.

Dedstorm's face filled the daytime sky.

"I'd have done it sooner," he whispered, "but I wanted to give you time to feed him, to help him recover. That way, you'd waste more time, and time is puzzle gun energy." He sighed. "I wish I could see your faces, but you've taken my eyes from me, destroyed my lovely deathhawk." Then, more loudly: "You've made me angry, Tinker!"

In an instant he was gone.

Tinker looked at the envoy's now lifeless form, then hung his head. He felt sick at heart and, for the first time, nearly hopeless.

* * *

Tinker's gaze took in the tranquil landscape as long shadows stretched from the hills into the City of the Ancients. In the still air, an unseen bird warbled its evening song. A few crickets began an early, lazy chirping.

Tinker, however, felt anything but tranquil. While Nirvana and Chameleon slept, exhausted with grief, Tinker had racked his brains for a plan. He still had no reasonable strategy for crossing the plain around the city.

At the edge of the city was a yawning chasm, which was the entrance to the arsenal of the Ancients. Dedstorm had already used Nirvana's memory cube to open it. Chameleon's cube would bring the drone army back to life.

In the shadows of that opening, Tinker saw row upon row of deadly silver machines. Chameleon's memory cube, if inserted in the abandoned guardhouse, could also destroy the army by triggering the self-destruct sequence. Dedstorm had left the guardhouse open. It was tempting bait.

"Have I failed?" Tinker wondered aloud. "I've tried my best to keep the team together. I didn't do that last time, and it was a disaster."

Last time? Twice now he had found himself talking this way. When had he faced a situation like this before?

Tinker shook his head. His entire life before the last few days was a blur. He remembered things here and there, but none of his memories were personal.

He looked up and said, "Chip!" Let there be at

least twenty percent power left, he thought. Twenty percent will give us a fighting chance.

"Go ahead."

"Puzzle gun status, please."

There was a brief pause. Finally the letters formed: "Batteries for the Logical Energy Processor are now at seven percent."

Tinker felt the blood drain from his face. Seven percent was nothing at all.

There was a sound to Tinker's right. He spun. It was Chameleon, joining him. "So what's the plan?"

"Wake Nirvana, and I'll tell you."

After Tinker's explanation, Chameleon said, "That's it?" She sat with her legs crossed, leaning against a tree. "That's the best you can do?"

"It could work," Nirvana said.

Chameleon considered for a few moments. "It depends too much on luck."

"It also depends on how fast we can run," Nirvana said.

"And on how close we can all get to the arsenal before Dedstorm sees us," Tinker added. "I know it's risky, but Dedstorm won't be able to concentrate his forces. And he won't use cyborgs here—it has to be wraiths. The poisons in the abandoned city would kill cyborgs in short order—and will kill us if we linger."

Chameleon gave him a skeptical look. She had guessed, Tinker realized, that the energy supply for the puzzle gun was nearly zero.

Chameleon's eyes narrowed, then she looked

away. "Well," she said, "I don't have a better plan to offer." She looked up again. "It will work. It has to."

Nirvana said, "How do we decide which of us will be the decoys? Who's really going to carry the memory cube?"

"We'll decide that by chance," Tinker said. He took three wide, soft leather straps from the inside of his tinker's vest. "Chameleon will find two stones about the size and shape of the memory cube, and then she'll wrap them and the cube with these straps. We'll each pick a package and carry it without knowing whether it's the cube or just a piece of ordinary rock."

"Why bother?" Chameleon asked.

Nirvana understood. "Dedstorm will watch us to see who is acting like a decoy and who isn't. But if we don't know ourselves, we can't give the secret away."

"Dedstorm can still generate many energy wraiths," Chameleon said. "There's no way that all three of us will make it to the guardhouse of the arsenal."

"That's true," Tinker admitted.

"In fact," Chameleon said, "chances are pretty poor for even one of us making it all the way, aren't they?"

Tinker didn't answer that.

"A one-in-three chance to save the galaxy. At best." Chameleon stood up. "I'll go find the rocks, and I'll try to find lucky ones."

* * *

Two hours after the sun had set, Tinker crouched in a bush at the edge of the plain, waiting for the others to get into place. They would make their move before the moon rose, counting on the darkness to hide them.

Now, Tinker thought, stepping out from the sheltering bushes. He held the puzzle gun, configured to Radiate and Focus. He would have liked to have used the Amplify cylinder, but Dedstorm had it.

One hundred yards to his left, he could see the dim shape of Nirvana also stepping out of cover. Chameleon would be another hundred yards beyond her.

Gripping the puzzle gun tightly, Tinker started to run toward the arsenal's guardhouse. He could feel the weight of the leather-wrapped object inside his vest. It was either the memory cube or a useless stone. He didn't want to know which until he had a chance, possibly, to use the cube.

Even in starlight, the City of the Ancients gleamed. So did Dedstorm's broken-glass towers. The uneven ground at Tinker's feet, however, was pitch-black.

"I wish there was just a little more light," Tinker spoke aloud.

Suddenly the sky was illuminated with the holographic projection of Dedstorm's face.

"I had to ask," Tinker said, and kept running. The glow from Dedstorm's face did at least make it easier for him to see where he was going.

"The sensors in my castle can be my eyes now!"

hissed Dedstorm. He furrowed his brow as though studying a chessboard from above. "Trying to divide my defenses? A strategy born of desperation, I'd say."

Let Dedstorm talk all he wants, Tinker thought. The more he talks, the closer we can get to the arsenal.

"What if I concentrate my forces?" Dedstorm said. "What if I send several wraiths after, let me see . . ."

Yellow light streaked from Dedstorm's castle.

"Let's make it Chameleon, shall we?"

The streaks of light landed, and Tinker saw that the wizard was suddenly surrounded by four energy wraiths. On this barren plain, far from living plants, she was powerless.

Tinker stopped running and dropped to one knee. He leveled the puzzle gun and fired four short bursts. Four times his energy pulses hit the target. The wraiths stopped and flickered but didn't wink out.

Chameleon dodged and kept running. Nirvana hadn't paused.

Dedstorm's image frowned. "Who has the memory cube, hmm? Tinker acts as though Chameleon does, but Nirvana runs as if she has it herself."

Four streaks from the castle touched down around Nirvana. She dealt with two of them, and Tinker zapped the other two. This time, both the wraiths he hit vanished. Dedstorm's energy must be running low, he thought, his heart surging with a sudden hope.

Chameleon kept running toward the guard-house, four dim wraiths still on her heels.

"You're not making this at all easy," Dedstorm said with the slightest trace of unease in his voice. His hologram flickered.

He's worried, Tinker realized. Maybe we have a chance!

He raced for the guardhouse.

"But I don't need to figure it out," Dedstorm said. "If I stop all three of you permanently, I can just search your lifeless bodies for the cube, can't I?"

Tinker didn't like the sound of that. And he didn't like the looks of what he saw coming, either, even if at first glance they appeared a little comical.

Rolling from the abandoned buildings of the City of the Ancients was a wave of three-wheeled vehicles. They had low, scoop-shaped bodies. To Tinker they resembled motorized wheelbarrows.

"Meet my newest invention," Dedstorm proudly announced, "and no arguments from you, Nirvana. This really is my invention. The portable death cage."

Tinker estimated that there were a hundred of the things, and they were fast. Tinker configured his puzzle gun to repel, and he took aim. When he pulled the trigger, a bolt of energy knocked over several of the strange machines, sending parts flying.

"Not very sturdy, are they?" Tinker said, although Dedstorm couldn't hear him. He took aim again.

Click.

Nothing happened. Tinker's worst fear had come true—the puzzle gun was out of power.

The first line of wheelbarrows rolled up to Chameleon. The wizard easily dodged them. Then three of her wraiths winked out, giving Tinker renewed hope. So Dedstorm's energy supply isn't limitless after all, he thought.

Tinker flung his now useless device aside and reached into his vest for what was either a rock or the memory cube. Without looking, he unwound the leather strap as he ran. Once or twice he felt a sharp edge, but he still couldn't be sure what the object was. Finally he got it unwrapped and felt six smooth sides—he had the memory cube.

More of the wheelbarrow machines came rolling forward, but judging from the ease with which both Chameleon and Nirvana dodged them, Tinker didn't feel very threatened. The main problem with the things, it seemed, was that they slowed you down. Some death cage, Tinker thought.

A small group of the little machines surged toward Tinker's shins. With one hand, he shoved them aside.

Then Tinker and the others discovered an even more irritating trait of the little machines. After they had dodged them, the machines came at them from behind, driving toward the back of their knees.

Chameleon was the first to fall. She had almost made her way to the arsenal's guardhouse when one of the machines tripped her up. The wizard fell backward into the wheelbarrow's bin.

Instantly bars of yellow energy leapt up from the sides of the bin—Chameleon was caged. With her elbows, she knocked at the glowing bars, but they held.

Dedstorm's image flickered again, then disappeared.

Tinker paused long enough to see the bars of Chameleon's cage shrink closer to her body, pinning her down. The last wraith reached for her but vanished before it could grab her.

Nirvana fell next, a lattice of energy quickly caging her in.

Now the little machines were bumping into Tinker from all sides. He staggered forward, clutching the precious memory cube tightly in his right hand. Over and over the thought pounded in his brain: I have to get to the arsenal. I can't let Dedstorm win.

He was close now—close enough to see the arsenal control panel, close enough to see the place where the cube would fit and to read the word Self-destruct.

Just a little farther, he told himself. A little farther and the galaxy will be saved.

A wheelbarrow hit him. He staggered, then caught himself.

Just a few steps more, Tinker told himself.

As if they were synchronized, three barrows hit

him in quick succession. He flailed his arms, fighting for balance.

Then, with a thump, he fell.

Yellow bars of solid energy closed above him, then shrank down against his body. Only his right arm dangled outside the cage.

Tinker looked past the bars at the memory cube in his hand. A rainbow of light shifted across its surface.

The bars shrank closer still, tightening against his chest. Tinker struggled to breathe.

The remaining wheelbarrows rolled aside to make way for someone who came walking out of the City of the Ancients.

"Do you see why I call it a death cage?"

"Dedstorm," Tinker managed to gasp. "Or another hologram?"

"Oh, it's the real me." Dedstorm smiled. "My energy's too low for holograms." He approached Tinker, and his hand closed around the memory cube. "I'll take that now."

"No," Tinker whispered.

"You'll let go," Dedstorm told him, "when the cage crushes you to death." He adjusted a setting on his power belt. The cage bars drew tighter and tighter.

Tinker felt the weight straining his ribs. He fought to get a gulp of air into his lungs, just a taste of breath.

The world started to go black. He felt his fingers loosen against his will.

118

"Goodbye, Tinker," he heard Dedstorm say. "I can't say I'll miss you."

No, no, no, Tinker thought. Not again! We *can't* lose!

Something in his body gave way painfully, and he slumped forward, crushed to death.

13

THE AIR IN FRONT OF TINKER GREW GRAINY. FLECKS of black, white, and gray danced before his eyes.

He took a breath. He could breathe! He was alive! But when he tried to get up, he couldn't. His head was still trapped.

Then he saw the words materialize in front of him in glowing green letters: Simulation Over.

Simulation?

He tried to look around, to orient himself, but something still held his head in place.

Then Tinker felt a switch under his hand. Instinctively he reached for it, even though he couldn't remember exactly what it was for. He toggled the switch.

Something rose slowly from his head—a helmet. He blinked as his eyes adjusted to the room light.

He looked down and noticed the shirt he was wearing. It was a cotton shirt, not a tinker's vest. Caltech, it read. Caltech? What was Caltech? And why hadn't Dedstorm killed him?

He stood up, took a wobbly step forward, and caught himself on the armrest of the strange chair he'd been sitting in.

On the other side of a glass wall he could see several control panels and a bank of glowing screens. Was this Dedstorm's castle?

"Where am I?" he said aloud.

"In laboratory D6, Swift Enterprises," said a mechanical voice.

Megatron, he thought blearily. And then, more certainly, he said, "Megatron!"

"Standing by," the computer said.

"I'm Tom Swift!" Tom said. "Tinker's a role-playing character! I'm alive!" He sat down on the side of the TRG chair. "It was a simulation!"

"Affirmative," Megatron said.

Of course! Tom rubbed his forehead. He was Tom Swift. He had been testing his latest invention, the Total Reality Generator, by running a depressingly real simulation. Tinker and his friends had died.

Tom stretched. He felt stiff. Then he realized he'd been inside the Galaxy Masters universe for more than two days of game time. How long had that been in the real world? He glanced up at the control room's twenty-four-hour clock.

Oh-six-hundred. He recalled that he'd started the simulation running at about two A.M. It had taken four hours, and now it was six o'clock. He had to be on his way to school in ninety minutes. He jumped up. I'm going to be a wreck today, Tom thought. And what about the Galaxy Masters tournament? I won't be able to think straight without any sleep.

Then he noticed that, aside from his stiffness, he didn't feel at all weary. He didn't have the slightest urge to yawn or lie down.

"Megatron," he ordered, "I want to record a lab note."

"Recording."

"Question: Can time in the TRG substitute for sleep? If so, make sure to study applications such as sleep learning. Perhaps pilots, astronauts, and deep-sea drill operators can train at night without losing any work time. Suggests whole new meaning for 'night school.' "

Tom grinned. What a discovery this could be!

Then the grin froze on his face. He still had two problems. First, no matter how wonderful the potential applications of the TRG might be, if he couldn't solve Megatron's power surge problem in the next thirty-six hours, he'd have to pull the fuzzy logic circuits that made the TRG possible.

The second problem, of course, was Galaxy Masters. The simulation seemed to confirm that Gary Gitmoe couldn't be beaten. Whatever strategy Tom tried against Gary's divide-and-conquer schemes, Dedstorm would still have the edge. As Alan had feared, Gary was unstoppable.

*　　*　　*

"But there has to be *some* way to stop him," Rick Cantwell said at lunch.

"Unless," Maria Santana said, "the game is flawed."

"Which seems likely," Tom added. "We're still testing Galaxy Masters, after all, so we shouldn't be surprised that it turns out to have some bugs."

"That's not going to matter to Dan," Mandy said gloomily. "Flawed game or not, Dan's still going to idolize Gary Gitmoe."

"I want to hear more about the TRG simulation," Alan Lee told Tom. "It sounds like Megatron did a great job of figuring out the game."

Tom smiled. "Megatron did more than figure out the game." He told the others about Rick's bottomless stomach, the heads-up display, and Dan Coster's band being incorporated into the TRG's version of the game.

"Prince Satori," Mandy said, rolling her eyes. "Give me a break."

"But didn't all those changed details also alter the game?" Alan asked.

"Not significantly," Tom said. "Megatron assured us of that, remember? But they did make for an interesting adventure, especially when I thought it was all really happening." His expression grew sober as he remembered how convincingly Megatron had cast Dedstorm as Tom's old enemy, the Black Dragon. The Black Dragon's habit of using holograms as masks was a chilling trait. Holograms wouldn't work that way in the real Galaxy Masters, though the rules did allow Dedstorm to project huge holograms into the sky.

"But we'd better forget the TRG for now," Tom said. "What do we do about this afternoon's match?"

Mandy pushed her cafeteria tray toward the center of the table. "Maybe Gary's team knows what to do. If Alan, playing Dedstorm for us, uses Gary's strategy against Gary's own team, and both games are being played simultaneously, then we can take our cue from Team Gitmoe."

"Good idea," Rick said. "Do you want that cake?"

Mandy shook her head, and Rick took the slice of pink-frosted layer cake from her tray.

"Don't you ever worry about getting fat?" Maria asked.

"I'm an athlete," Rick said. "I burn up every calorie I eat."

"Mandy's idea *is* a good one," said Alan. "If Gary's strategy has a flaw, his teammates should know what it is."

"If they don't," Tom said, "what are we going to do?"

"You'll figure something out, Tom," Rick said. "You always do." He turned to Alan. "Are you going to finish those french fries?"

"Rick, you eat like an alien," Tom said.

"So what's our opening strategy going to be?" Maria asked, "before we figure out what Gary's teammates are doing against Alan?"

"Well," Tom said, "I think the simulation revealed how we can use a weakness in Gary's personality. He isn't just playing to win, he's playing to humiliate us."

Rick nodded. "You said it."

"The Dedstorm in the TRG is modeled after Gary's style of play. And in the simulation, Dedstorm used up a lot of energy taunting Tinker's team. I can easily imagine Gary doing the same thing. If we can get him to waste energy bragging, then maybe he'll deplete his energy supply enough for us to have a chance."

"See?" Rick said, stuffing in another fry. "I knew you'd come up with something!"

Tom didn't think this idea alone would be enough to defeat Gary, but he kept his thoughts to himself. He was the leader. Even if things looked bad, he didn't want his teammates to be discouraged.

When Tom returned to the cafeteria a few hours later, the scene was different altogether. It seemed as if every student from Jefferson High was staying after school to watch the championship match of Galaxy Masters. Gary Gitmoe must have been spreading the word that he would wipe out his opponents in a particularly awesome fashion.

Two tables in the center of the room were reserved for the players. At one table, Les Hempel ran the computer that would help him referee the game between Tom's heroes and Gary's Dedstorm. At the other table, Mr. Hempel waited with an identical computer to referee the game in which

Alan would play Dedstorm against Dan Coster as Tinker, Bob Wolf as the Denebian envoy, Jessica Trine as Chameleon, and Tracy Shaw as Princess Nirvana. Two more computers stood ready for the secret moves of the two Dedstorms.

All of Gary's teammates were already in the room, talking to the spectators in a relaxed way as if they expected an easy victory.

Tom worked his way through the crowd, accepting wishes of luck from both friends and others he hardly knew. He sat down in the empty chair between Rick and Mandy. A moment later Maria joined them. From the other end of the table, Gary Gitmoe looked up and smiled with contempt.

The room was a buzz of conversations. Tom picked out a sentence or two here and there, speculations on who would win. It seemed that Gary's team was the favorite.

"Can you believe the size of this crowd?" Maria said.

"Remember," Mandy told the others, keeping her voice low, "we've got to keep track of what Gary's team is doing against Alan. That's how we'll want to play against Gary."

"And we're trying to get Gary to waste energy," Tom added.

"So," Gary Gitmoe said in a loud voice, "have you hatched some secret plan to defeat me?" He laughed. "It can't be something I haven't already thought of myself. You've met your match, believe me."

126

"No way, Gitmoe," Rick said. "We've got the world's most experienced Galaxy Masters player on our team."

Gary laughed. "Come on, Cantwell. Everybody here has played the same number of games."

"Except for Tom," Rick said mysteriously. "Our leader hasn't just played Galaxy Masters. He's *lived* it."

"Everybody ready?" Mr. Hempel asked. He clapped his hands, and the room grew quiet.

"Welcome to the first-ever championship of Galaxy Masters," Mr. Hempel said. "I expect this to be an interesting matchup." He looked over at his son's table, where Gary and Rick were glaring at each other.

"A couple of reminders. Please keep your voices down during play so that the participants can concentrate. If you aren't quiet, there's really no way that you can follow a role-playing game like this. All the action will take place in your imaginations as the players describe their moves and the referees—my son and I—announce the computer-generated consequences of those moves."

To Alan and Dan he said, "Shall we begin?" They nodded, and Mr. Hempel sat down behind his computer.

"Okay, Dedstorm," Mr. Hempel said to Alan. "What's your first move?"

Alan typed a secret move on the keyboard. Mr. Hempel read it, typed something into his own keyboard, and told Dan Coster, "Tinker, four of Ded-

storm's energy wraiths have just flashed down and
are attacking."

"Energy wraiths already?" Dan said. "Alan
never used energy wraiths this early in his other
games."

"But this is what we expected him to do," Bob
Wolf said, smiling.

At the other table, Les asked, "Are you guys
ready to start, too?"

Gary nodded and typed in a move. "Where have
I seen Alan's strategy used before, Tom?"

At the first table, Mr. Hempel announced, "Two
of the wraiths move in on Chameleon."

"I'm aiming the puzzle gun at a wraith," said
Dan Coster, "and I pull the trigger."

"A bolt of energy shoots out and hits the
wraith," said Mr. Hempel. "The wraith dims very
slightly."

"What?" Dan said. "Oh, yeah, I've got to put the
right cylinders in the thing."

"Okay, guys," Les Hempel said to the players at
the other table. "Here we go." He read Gary's
move from the computer screen. "Dedstorm is
sending four energy wraiths to attack you."

"Not very original," Maria quipped.

"It's my strategy," Gary snapped. "Alan ripped it
off."

"Alan didn't rip anything off," said Tracy Shaw
from the other table. She was standing up, too
intent on the game to sit. "Using somebody else's
strategy is part of any game." Then to Mr. Hempel, she said, "Nirvana sneaks up on the other

wraith that's attacking Chameleon. She hits it from behind with her bracers."

"The wraith falls to its knees. As it falls it reaches for Nirvana's legs," Mr. Hempel reported.

Tracy jumped back from the table, almost knocking over a pair of spectators. Laughter. "I dodge," she said.

"Not quite quickly enough," Mr. Hempel told her, still reading from the screen. "Nirvana has a bad wraith burn on her right leg."

Bob Wolf spoke up. "The envoy grabs two of the wraiths and destroys them."

"Okay, I've got the puzzle gun put together," Dan said. "I'm using Amplify, Radiate, and Focus. I'll shoot the wraith who's going after Nirvana first."

"Zap!" Mr. Hempel said. "The wraith is gone."

"It doesn't matter if Alan uses my strategy," Gary smugly told Tom's team. "I've thought it all through. You can't win."

"If your strategy is so unstoppable," Mandy said, "then why are your teammates acting as if they have a plan to beat it?"

"Oh, my team has a plan, all right. Wait and see."

Les reminded Tom's team that they'd better start dealing with the wraiths that had just arrived.

"Right," Tom said. He visualized his puzzle gun elements, then announced that he was building a weapon like the one that Dan was using in the other game.

129

"Not very original," Dan mimicked Maria. Then he said to Mr. Hempel, "I'm trying to zap the last wraith."

"Got it," said Mr. Hempel. "All the attacking wraiths are gone. Nobody on your side is hurt, and you've got ninety-five percent of your puzzle gun's power."

"Come on, Tinker," Rick said. "Zap those wraiths!"

"I aim and fire," Tom said.

"Zap!" Les said. "That's one gone."

Mandy, meanwhile, was paying close attention to what was happening with Gary's group. "Hey!" she said. "Gary's team just called out a weird move. Dan said that they're exposing their memory cubes and placing them on the ground."

"I'm aiming the puzzle gun at the cubes," Dan said, "and now I pull the trigger."

Mr. Hempel gave Dan a curious look.

"We can do that, can't we?" Dan asked.

"You can," Mr. Hempel said. "I just don't know why you would." He keyed in the move. "The memory cubes vanish in a flash of multicolored light." He looked up. "And the game is over. With both cubes destroyed, neither Dan's heroes nor Alan's Dedstorm can win. It's a draw."

"All right!" Dan cheered, as if his team had just won.

"I don't get it," said a voice in the crowd. "Why'd you do that?"

"Isn't it obvious?" Gary said, raising his voice above the murmuring crowd.

The spectators grew silent.

"I have an unbeatable strategy," Gary explained. "Once my team confirmed that Alan was using it, they forced the best possible outcome—a draw."

Rick said, "But I still don't—"

"You're slow on the uptake, aren't you, Cantwell?" Gary said. "On Friday Les announced that my team had an edge going into this final game. So to win the tournament now, all I have to do is force a draw." He grinned. "The only way you can keep me from winning the championship is by winning this match. And I've already told you: My strategy is unbeatable."

14

THE ROOM BUZZED WITH CONVERSATION, AND Mr. Hempel had to remind the spectators to be quiet.

Tom narrowed his eyes, thinking about what had just happened. Gary had introduced a new wrinkle into the game. How could Tom and his teammates take advantage of it?

As he stared intently into the empty space above the table, Tom saw himself standing alongside the envoy, Nirvana, and Chameleon. Brush-covered hills rose in front of him. Waves tumbled onto the beach. "Here's what we have to do," Tom said as he began to live the game. . . .

"Here's what we have to do," Tinker told the others, facing the hills. The breeze from the sea tossed his blond hair. "We can't give Dedstorm the slightest chance of winning. We have to keep the arsenal of the Ancients out of his reach."

"But how?" asked the envoy, whose face switched back and forth between his blue features and Rick's human face as Tom/Tinker's concentration waxed and waned.

"Nirvana," Tinker said, "put your memory cube down on the ground and stand back from it."

Nirvana did so, and Tinker looked up at the sky. High above, a dot circled.

"Here's hoping the deathhawk gets an eyeful of this," Tinker said. He aimed the puzzle gun at the cube and fired. . . .

"So you fried Nirvana's cube." Gary shook his head. "I thought you'd at least keep things interesting."

"We still have Chameleon's cube," Tom said, "and that's all we need to destroy the arsenal. Now either *we* win or *you* force a draw and win the championship. But you can't win outright."

"That's not very sporting," Gary complained.

"You should talk," Rick said.

"Sporting or not," said Mr. Hempel, looking at his son, "it's not very good game design. I'm afraid we have some bugs to work out, Les."

Les nodded thoughtfully. "Maybe we haven't balanced the game as well as we thought."

"It doesn't matter," Gary said with a wave of his hand. "We've all played the same number of matches by the same rules. I'll win because I analyzed the game better than anyone else." He tapped something into his keyboard, then looked at Tom. "Here come more energy wraiths to drain Tinker's batteries."

"More wraiths!" Chameleon cried.

"Dedstorm's really turning up the heat!" the envoy said, grabbing a wraith by the neck.

Yellow energy sparked and crackled from the struggling wraith and coursed over the envoy's body. He seized another wraith and began to drain the energy from it. But now his hands were full. More wraiths surrounded him, trying to lift him from the ground.

"No!" Tinker cried, firing the puzzle gun and vaporizing two wraiths. "Dedstorm's trying to kidnap the envoy again!"

Nirvana, swinging her forearms, stepped into the fray, sending wraiths leaping back from her bracers. Sparks flew as the metal on her wrists struck and destroyed a wraith.

Chameleon waved her hands and made a dozen bushes grow into a wooden cage over the envoy, keeping the wraiths from flying off with him.

But still more wraiths came streaking down from the eastern sky. They grabbed onto the envoy even as the first ones he had seized winked out of existence.

Tinker raised his puzzle gun and fired. "I don't like this one bit," he said. "We're a long way from the City of the Ancients, and my batteries are draining."

"Tinker!" Nirvana shouted, pointing. A wraith that had slipped behind Chameleon opened its arms for a deadly embrace.

Tinker aimed and pulled the trigger. The wraith winked out. "More precious energy gone," he said grimly.

"Then do something!" the envoy cried. "Don't you have a plan?"

"Whoa, Tom!" Rick said, waving his hand in front of Tom's face. "Snap out of it!"

"He's just concentrating," Mandy said.

"His eyes are glazing over."

Dan Coster snickered. "Yo, Tom-Tom. Is Tinker seeing his life flash before his eyes?"

Tom blinked. "I'm okay, Envoy," he said to Rick. "You're right. We have a plan. Let's use it. You just keep draining down those wraiths. Dedstorm can't keep them coming forever."

"You bet," Rick agreed. "I can handle them."

"I've got you where I want you, Swift," Gary taunted.

Tom seemed to surface a little from his trance. "Tinker can't hear Dedstorm," Tom said, "so I can't hear a word you're saying."

"All I'm saying—" Gary started to say.

Tom cut him off. "I fire at another wraith."

"Another one down," Les said. "The wraiths are beginning to run out of energy. One by one, they wink out."

"All I'm saying—"

"Sorry, Gary," Tom said. "Can't hear you."

135

"Then I'll fix it so you have to listen. Les, can Dedstorm talk to Tinker?"

"He can if he projects a hologram into the sky. That uses energy, though, and you used most of your reserve creating those wraiths."

"I don't care," Gary said.

Tom carefully hid his smile. Then he narrowed his eyes again to concentrate.

"The last three wraiths wink out together," Les said. "Dedstorm's energy is way down."

Mr. Hempel watched Tom with interest, but Tom barely noticed him. Instead, he kept staring into space at the low hills and the mountains beyond. There was a cleft far ahead, a canyon . . .

. . . a canyon with high walls.

"We're going to bypass the Canyon of the Ancients," Tinker said to his exhausted companions. "It's too easy for Dedstorm to set a trap there."

"Then we'll have to go over the mountains," Chameleon said. "That will take longer."

"And it'll be cold," Nirvana added. "We'll freeze."

"Don't worry," Tinker said, patting the puzzle gun. "I've thought about that."

As the group started over the hills, they were still miles from the mouth of the canyon. Dedstorm's deathhawk must have relayed the news of this unexpected route, because the evening sky suddenly lit up with the enormous holographic image of Dedstorm's face.

"Do you think it makes any difference what

route you take?" The image laughed evilly. "You can't defeat me, Tinker. None of your schemes will work. I have the edge, and I plan to exploit it!"

"*Do* we have a chance?" Chameleon asked. "Honestly, Tinker. What do you think?'

Tinker looked up at the face in the sky. "I'd say our chances are getting better all the time," he said. A dim flicker of light passed over the eye of Dedstorm's hologram. The deathhawk. "Of course," Tinker said, "there are still a few things we need to take care of."

"It won't help you," Gary said, "forcing me to use a hologram to talk to you. I'll still have energy to spare."

"We'll see," was all Tom said.

Gary shook his head. "You aren't going to psych me out, Tom Swift."

To Les, Tom said, "I'm going to make a device out of my tinker's gear, and I'm going to do it secretly, hunched over so that what I'm making can't be observed from the sky."

"Okay," Les said, starting to key the move into the computer. "What are you making?"

"Something out of nuts and bolts and a spool of copper wire. But if I tell you more than that, it won't be a secret, will it?" He diagrammed the device and wrote down how it would be used.

"I guess that would work," Les said, looking at the diagram.

"What is it?" asked Gary. There was a trace of uncertainty in his voice.

"Sorry, Dedstorm," Les said. "Tinker has succeeded in making this device in secret."

The cafeteria audience was silent, watching intently as Tom wrote another note and passed it to Rick. "I'm giving the envoy instructions on how to use the device," he said.

"Of the four of us," Tinker told the envoy, "you probably have the best throwing arm." He handed over the assembly of bolts and wire.

The blue alien grinned. "Well," he said, "I do have the best pass completion percentage in the history of Jefferson High football."

Tinker gave him a funny look. That seemed like a strange thing for the envoy to say.

"Make all the little toys you want to," Dedstorm grumbled from the sky. "You still can't win!"

"It will take a long time to get over the mountains," Les said. "Five days of game time, at least."

"Plenty of time for me to keep sending energy wraiths at your team," Gary said.

"So send them," Rick said.

"Uh-oh," Mandy said. "Tom's eyes are glazing over again."

"Of course," Alan called from his place at the other table. "The rest of you are just playing this game. Tom is living it."

It was snowing on the mountain pass as Tinker and his companions made their night crossing.

138

They had been traveling for three days now, dealing with an almost constant assault of energy wraiths. Now a frigid wind whipped around them fiercely.

"I'm freezing!" Nirvana complained.

"I'm cold, too," Tinker said. He started to change the configuration of his puzzle gun. The cylinders he inserted were Radiate, Disperse, and Shape.

"The envoy looks cold," Chameleon said, "but then he always looks cold with that blue skin of his."

"I'm not so much cold as hungry," the envoy grumbled.

"We'll be out of the wind soon," Tinker told them. "Then we'll stop to eat." He pulled the trigger of the puzzle gun. Instantly the four travelers were bathed in an orb of orange warmth.

"Ah," Nirvana said gratefully. "Much better!"

"What about the energy you're using?" Chameleon said.

"This isn't an amplified configuration," Tinker told her. "It does take some energy, but not much."

"This route is taking us forever," Nirvana said, "and your puzzle gun drains even when you don't use it."

True enough, Tinker thought. He had avoided a trap in the canyon by taking this route, but Nirvana was right. Time was against them.

Something blue flashed from the sky.

"Heads up, everyone," Tinker said. "Death-hawk!"

The robotic bird swept low through the swirling snow. It fired an energy bolt that shot wide. Then, flying beyond them, the bird began a wide turn that would bring it back toward Tinker and the others. For a moment it was invisible in the falling snow.

"What better time to attack?" boomed Dedstorm's voice. "The temperature is falling, Tinker. Defend yourself or freeze!"

"Keep a sharp eye out, Envoy," Tinker said. Off to one side, the falling snow glowed faintly blue. "Here it comes."

The deathhawk shot forward.

"Now, Envoy!" Tinker cried. "Now!"

As the mechanical wings appeared through the snowflakes, the envoy hurled Tinker's wire device into the deathhawk's path.

"And as soon as the spool unwinds and makes contact with the ground," Les said, "the death-hawk goes up in a lightning bolt and a cloud of smoke."

A cheer went up in the cafeteria.

"All right!" Rick said. He and Maria traded high fives.

"What?" Gary said, enraged.

"Time for a snack!" Rick said. "Let's celebrate." Everyone ignored him.

Gary was still fuming. "They can get away with that?"

140

"That is exactly the sort of thing Tinker is supposed to do," Mr. Hempel told him. "He's the creative linchpin of the team."

Gary scowled. "Okay, so they zapped my death-hawk. I don't care. I'm *still* unstoppable. I'm sending eight energy wraiths against them."

"That's too many," Les said, reading from the screen. "You don't have energy for more than five."

"All right, all right," Gary snapped. "Five, then."

"We're still going to win, Gary," Dan said. "Right?"

Gary ignored him.

"Five it is," Les said, and a battle was soon under way in the swirling snow. Tom watched it unfold.

The sun was coming up. Wet, exhausted, and hungry, the members of Tinker's team collapsed on the hillside.

"Chameleon's wraith burns look bad," Nirvana said.

"I'm okay," Chameleon said. "I'm just tired of constantly getting cut off and attacked."

"That's Dedstorm's strategy," Tinker reminded her, "to split us up or make us fight to stay together."

"What's your energy supply?" asked the envoy.

"Twenty percent," Tinker told him. "Fighting wraiths for four days has cost us."

"But we're almost there," Nirvana said. The

TOM SWIFT

Plain of the Ancients was visible from where they rested, and they could see the arsenal guardhouse, their goal.

"Maybe we should split up," Chameleon said. "Then Tinker could conserve his energy. We could give Tinker the cube to take the rest of the way."

"And have me face every wraith Dedstorm has left by myself?" Tinker said. "No, thanks!"

"Uh-oh," the envoy said. "See those streaks of light coming from Dedstorm's castle?"

"More wraiths," Nirvana groaned.

Tinker said, "We'll handle them."

"Well," Les said, after the wraiths were dispersed, "you've managed to keep your team together all the way to the Plain of the Ancients." He looked up at Tom. "And you've used all but one percent of your puzzle gun energy."

"That's it," Gary Gitmoe said. "You can't cross the plain without help from your puzzle gun. Especially," he added, tapping his move into the computer, "after you face five more wraiths."

"Four wraiths," Les corrected him. "Your energy is low."

"Whatever," Gary snapped. "I've won."

Maria groaned. "Oh, no. We've done everything right, and we're still going to lose."

Tom was staring at his hands, visualizing the puzzle gun. No way did he want to let his friends down, but what could he do with only a one percent charge?

15

WHILE TOM WAS LOST IN THOUGHT, RICK MADE his way through the crowd to the cafeteria's vending machines and returned with a candy bar.

"How can you eat at a time like this?" Maria asked.

"Just because we're all about to die is no reason to go hungry," Rick told her. He took a big bite.

"Well, at least you could eat a little more responsibly," Maria said, exasperated. "I mean, a candy bar?"

"This *is* responsible," Rick protested. "I'll have you know the wrapper is made from recycled paper."

"I wish the energy in Tinker's puzzle gun were recyclable," Mandy said glumly.

"Yeah," Maria agreed. "Or that we could recharge it with solar energy or something."

"Come on, Tom," Les said. "You need to come up with a move. What's Tinker going to do about these wraiths?"

"Recycle," Tom murmured. He concentrated and pictured the puzzle gun. "Recharge," he said.

"The puzzle gun can't be recharged," Les reminded him.

"At least we didn't program that into the game," Mr. Hempel added, watching Tom intently.

The faint smile on Tom's face grew wider. "Recycle," he said a little louder. "Recharge!"

Tom held his hands as though there were something in them, a device about a foot long. He cradled it like a gun.

"There's something in the game rules," Tom said, "about the official name of the puzzle gun. My simulation last night reminded me of it."

"Simulation? What simulation?" Mr. Hempel asked. But Tom was too absorbed to hear the question.

A full-fledged grin broke out on Tom's face. "The puzzle gun is also called the Logical Energy Processor."

"Right," Les said, "because that's what it does. The cylinders that go with the gun work by logic. There's nothing in existing science that really works that way."

Tom laughed, imagining the puzzle gun in his hands.

"All right," he said. "Here's my move."

His thumb moved a catch release that wasn't

really there, and his hand closed on an imaginary cylinder. "The puzzle gun is now configured as an antiwraith gun, with cylinders for Amplify...." He held up the imaginary cylinder so that everyone in the cafeteria, players and spectators alike, could "see" it. "Radiate . . ." He held up that cylinder. "And Focus."

"He'd better make his move in a hurry," Gary Gitmoe complained. "My wraiths are landing all around him."

"He's making it," Mr. Hempel said, watching Tom carefully. "He's making it."

"Now I'm putting the following cylinders back into the frame: first Focus, then Radiate, then Disperse. And I'm wrapping wire around the chamber of the gun to hold the cylinders in place."

"There's nothing new about that combination," Gary said. "It lets you shoot out a ray that you can manipulate like a rope."

"No," Mr. Hempel said, smiling. "You weren't watching closely enough. Before Tom—or should I say Tinker—put the Focus cylinder back into the frame, he turned it around. The green arrows are pointing the wrong way."

Tom nodded. "The same goes for the Radiate cylinder. Two cylinders point the wrong way. The Disperse cylinder doesn't. It should still form a broad field, but it's connected to a backward radiation cylinder. Instead of radiating, the cylinder should absorb energy, and the last cylinder focuses the absorbed energy onto my power supply."

145

"But the cylinders aren't designed to fit in backward," Les objected.

"That's why I'm using the wire to hold them in place."

"Even so, it won't work," Les said. "That's not something we programmed into the game."

"Nice try, Swift," Gary said. "You lose."

"Not so fast," Mr. Hempel said. "Les, go ahead and key Tom's move into the computer."

"But the game isn't programmed for this!"

"No," Mr. Hempel said. "But we did program the software to handle the puzzle gun as a logic problem, and we gave it certain rules to work by. Let's see what happens."

"I point the puzzle gun at the nearest wraith," Tom said, swinging the imagined device around, "and I pull the trigger."

Reluctantly Les typed in the commands. "It's not going to do anything," he predicted.

"Yes, it is," Mr. Hempel said, reaching past his son to point at the computer screen. "Look!"

"One of the wraith icons just vanished," Les said. He keyed in something else. "Let me check— Hey! Puzzle gun energy is up to three percent! It worked!"

"Tinker aims at another wraith and fires," Tom said.

Les's fingers flew over the keyboard. "Zap!" he said. "Two down, two to go. Energy back to five percent!"

"All right!" Maria shouted.

"Go, Tom!" Mandy cheered.

"I'm pulling back the two remaining wraiths," Gary said. "I'm not going to let Tinker recharge his gun!"

"Okay," Les said, "but what *are* you going to do? Anything you might use against Tinker on the Plain of the Ancients uses the same energy that powers his puzzle gun. The only exception was your electronic deathhawk."

"Oh, shut up!" Gary snapped.

"I was only trying to explain—"

Gary shoved his chair back from the table. "I'm not going to finish this stupid game."

"Come on, Gary," Tracy Shaw urged. "Be a sport for once. And what about the rest of us?"

Gary turned to glare at her.

"Maybe you can counter Tinker's new power," Les said.

"Who cares? It's only a stupid game!" Gary got up and stormed out of the cafeteria. There were a few quiet boos from the spectators as he left.

Dan Coster looked stunned.

"Just to tie things up," Tom said, "my team crosses the Plain of the Ancients and inserts the memory cube in the guardhouse. We activate the self-destruct sequence."

"There's no one to stop you," Les said. "The ground shakes, and as the army of the Ancients melts down, the city crumbles into dust." He looked up from the screen. "The galaxy is safe. Game over. You win."

The crowd erupted in cheers as Alan shouted, "Way to go, Tinker!"

Tracy Shaw came over from the other table and offered her hand. "Congratulations."

"Yeah, good going, Tom," said Jessica.

Bob Wolf also came over to shake Tom's hand. "Hey, Swift," he said. "Gary told us you were boring and predictable. He was wrong." He paused. "Gary's reaction to losing—now, *that* was boring and predictable."

Then Tom's gaze met Dan Coster's. Dan's face was red, and he seemed about to look away. Tom stuck out his hand. "You play a good Tinker," Tom said.

"You play a better one," Dan admitted. He hesitated, then shook Tom's hand. "I guess I'm not as good at picking winners as I thought I was."

"It's not just a matter of picking winners," Rick said. "It's a question of how you play the game."

"Yeah," Dan mumbled. He was quiet for a moment. Then he turned away from the table.

"Where are you going?" Mandy asked.

"There's someone I need to talk to," Dan said. "Ed Griffy. The Scavengers could use a second rhythm guitar."

Mandy gave Tom's hand a surreptitious squeeze under the table. Tom felt his face redden, but he turned and smiled at her.

"Well, it seems our game needs some more design work," Mr. Hempel said.

Les turned off the computer. "Does it ever! First it looked like Dedstorm might have an unfair advantage. Now it turns out that Tinker does."

"Not unfair, exactly," Mr. Hempel said. "Remember all the players who didn't think to try what Tom tried."

"I know, I know," Les said. "But now that Tom has done it, everybody else who plays the game will turn the cylinders around the wrong way. We have to give Dedstorm some kind of balancing abilities."

"Well, we'll get around to that. Game design is like anything else that's creative. If you fall down, you get up and try again." He turned to Tom. "You worked with the puzzle gun almost as if you could see it in your hands."

"It *was* real for him," Alan said. "Tom has invented a machine called the Total Reality Generator that lets you see, feel, and hear your simulated surroundings. We programmed it to play Galaxy Masters."

"Really!" Mr. Hempel looked surprised. "Tom, this simulator sounds like the kind of system I've always dreamed of for role-playing games. There could be big money in this."

"Actually," Tom said, "the TRG is supposed to be a serious training simulator. As far as commercial applications go, there are some bugs to work out."

"Bugs?"

"Glitches serious enough that the TRG is headed for the scrap heap, unless I can figure out something fast," Tom said. "The fuzzy logic circuits that make it work are causing power surges at Swift Enterprises. Our supercomputer, Megatron, has lost the ability to control electricity with subtlety. It says it can't feel what it's doing. If I don't fix the problem soon, we'll have to shut down the TRG."

"Maybe you could work on it somewhere else," said Mr. Hempel. "Perhaps we could build facilities."

"No other computer in the world comes close to matching Megatron." Tom sighed. "I'm afraid it's Swift Enterprises or nowhere for the TRG."

"That's too bad," Mr. Hempel said. He smiled a little sadly. "Maybe the TRG is just too good to be true."

"I really want to solve Megatron's problem," Tom said, "but I've only got twenty-four hours."

"Sounds kind of hopeless," Les said.

"It's clear from the way you played," Mr. Hempel said, "that your simulator trained your whole body for the game. You didn't just play the game. You were there."

"Of course," Tom said. "That's because in the TRG, my whole body feels—" He stopped in midsentence. "My whole body *feels*," he repeated.

For long seconds, Tom stared into space.

"Tom, buddy?" Rick said. "Tom?"

"His eyes are glazing over," Mandy warned.

"His fingers are twitching!" said Maria.

"He's smiling," Alan said.

Rick announced, "He's inventing something!"

"I could give Megatron a simulated body!" Tom said. "Instead of a binary nervous system, it could have a 'real' one, using the TRG itself! Megatron would be able to detect all the subtle changes it's been missing!"

Mr. Hempel looked hopeful. "Does that mean—"

"Come on, guys," Tom said, standing up in a hurry. "See you later, Mr. Hempel."

"But what about—"

"Later, Mr. Hempel! Later!"

Rick, Mandy, Maria, and Alan finally caught up with Tom at the gate of Swift Enterprises. He practically flew into the laboratory wing that housed the TRG. He paused at the handprint recognition panel just long enough for it to open the first security doors.

"What musical artist—" the voice recognition system began, but Tom cut it off with, "Bob Dylan! Prince! Madonna! Open the door!"

Recognizing his voice pattern, the system complied. Tom dashed to the control room consoles, turned on a monitor, and started to key in circuit-routing instructions.

Out of breath, his four friends followed.

"Megatron," Tom said after working for a few minutes, "do you understand the purpose of this circuit adjustment?"

"Affirmative," the computer replied.

"Then complete the task," Tom said.

The circuit diagram on the screen squirmed like a plate of worms. Mandy leaned over Tom's shoulder, watching.

"There you have it," Tom said when the diagram had stopped changing. "Meet the new Mega-tron, complete with an analog nervous system."

"Which means what?" Mandy asked.

"Megatron will regulate its energy control the way our nervous systems regulate us," Alan guessed. "Right, Tom?"

Tom keyed in a query at the keyboard, and Megatron answered, "Probability of power surges is now zero."

Tom smiled. "We can continue to perfect the TRG. One of these days, it's going to live up to its name and be a perfect, *total* reality generator."

Mandy leaned over and kissed Tom.

"Um," Tom said, grinning and feeling his face flush at the same time. "What was that for?"

"Just a reminder, Tom Swift," Mandy said with a smile, "that there are still some things a machine just can't duplicate."

Tom's next adventure:

Something fishy is going on down at Laguna Pequeña beach. The ocean has turned into an aquatic nightmare. A grotesque giant squid, a hideous herring with razor-sharp teeth, and a gruesome fifty-foot shark have laid siege to the shore—and many lay the blame on Tom Swift's latest oceanic research!

Tom is using growth hormones to create huge fish, hoping to help feed starving people around the world. Convinced that his experiment is safe, he believes that the true source of the beasts from the deep lies elsewhere. Tom also suspects that a deranged scientist is about to take one more horrifying step: the genetic alteration of human beings . . . in Tom Swift #11, *Mutant Beach*.